CHASING NATE

CHASING NATE

A R ZERBY

KITTELSON PRESS
FARMINGTION TOWNSHIP

COPYRIGHT 2019 by A R Zerby

All rights reserved

KDP ISBN:9781091595071

Imprint:Independently published

WWW.CHASINGNATE.COM

author@chasingnate.com

This project is dedicated to my wife Bonnie and our children. Without you, this wouldn't be possible. All my love
 Alan

Cover design - Lisa Zerby

CONTENTS

One	**VERY BAD THINGS**
Two	**HIDE IT**
Three	**LYING DICKWEED**
Four	**WHOA**
Five	**NO MAIL NO CUTLASS**
Six	**SISTERS**
Seven	**SHE'S DEAD!**
Eight	**RUNAWAY EXPRESS**
Nine	**GOOBER'S AUTO**
Ten	**DO THE MATH**
Eleven	**BOLO FOR THE LEO**
Twelve	**MINNE-SNOWDA**
Thirteen	**BRIGHT LIGHTS DASH LIGHTS**
Fourteen	**SOME BACHELOR PARTY**
Fifteen	**LONG DAY**

Sixteen	**CONVOY**
Seventeen	**BUMPER CARS**
Eighteen	**GREAT BALLS OF FIRE**
Nineteen	**EVOLUTION**
Twenty	**OW MY HEAD!**
Twenty One	**FINDING AUNT TRACI**
Twenty Two	**FIRST NEWS**
Twenty Three	**THIS ISN'T A JOKE?**
Twenty Four	**WIPE DOWN THE CAR**
Twenty Five	**B & E**
Twenty Six	**CONTACT!**
Twenty Seven	**WHAT ARE THE ODDS?**
Twenty Eight	**THEM PESKY KIDS**
Twenty Nine	**BUCKLE UP TOOTS!**
Thirty	**NOW WHAT?**

CHAPTER ONE

VERY BAD THINGS

Two very bad things were aimed at Angus 'Blackie' MacDonald as he stood shivering on the highway shoulder that miserable December morning. A southeast wind pelted his jacket with sleet and blew it down his neck as he peered across the blacktop. Yup, there was mail. He turned his head left and pulled the thick stocking cap tighter over his ears.

A mile away, to the north, the first bad thing appeared. He watched as a semi crested the hilltop and saw the vehicle slowly but steadily pick up speed as it approached the curve at the bottom.

"Holy cow dude, slow down!"

Blackie unconsciously started inching back up his driveway, unable to look away from the drama unfolding in front of him. This could be bad he thought.

Inside the Kenworth, the trucker's eyes popped open. He quickly took in his speed, the icy road and the curve.

"SHIT!"

The entire rig teetered on the edge of the driver's control

as he held his foot just above the brake. He spotted the figure on the side of the road and put out a quick, silent prayer for the man's safety. A gentle adjustment of the steering wheel to the right would hopefully bring his tires back from the shoulder.

The ass end of the trailer started to break free but slowly, ever so slowly, got in line with the tractor. The driver eased the eighteen-wheeler back into the southbound lane as his heart hammered in his chest. He successfully negotiated the curve and was still slowing, as he sprayed a cold wet wave against the figure on the highway's edge.

Blackie thought 'Yeah, you better slow down', now wetter and colder, but also relieved. He took another look in both directions, then crossed to the mailbox. With his back to the wind, he pulled out a bundle of letters and bills. Another traffic check and Angus started back, shuffling thru the mail as he crossed the highway. On his way back to the warmth of his kitchen, the second bad thing revealed itself.

One largish envelope was addressed to his son Nate, with a handwritten return address. From Las Vegas.

"This can't be good."

Angus remembered the scene two weeks earlier when he

and Nate had some harsh words for each other in the kitchen.

"I hate living out here in the middle of nowhere. It sucks!"

The boy scowled at his father across the kitchen table.

"Yeah, we're in the country, not in town. We're in the boonies. That's just how it is son."

Nate rolled his eyes at that.

"But I've never turned you down for a ride to town. Never!"

The microwave dinged to signal supper was ready. Leftovers. Angus moved to dish up their meal but he kept on talking.

"You're close to getting your license. License means freedom."

Nate shook his head, started to leave, fleeing the coming conversation that he could script in his head. His Dad moved behind the boy and reached out, gently put his hand on Nate's shoulder. Blackie spoke again, in a more measured tone.

"If you play your cards right, be just a little easier to get along with, focus on school a little more, you'll get a set of wheels. Independence ya know?"

Blackie thought that was a logical, compelling argument.

"Yeah, you'll probably give me that piece of shit truck of yours!" Nate snarled as he sprang away.

Dear old Dad was caught off-guard and did a double-take. 'WUT? Dissing my ride?'

"My God, wouldn't want you to stoop so low as to have to drive THAT! For free too!"

The calm, adult voice was gone, replaced with a snarl. His button was pushed.

Nate stomped off. The SLAM of his bedroom door marked the end of another dinner hour, an all-too frequent occurrence recently.

Angus snapped back to the chilly present, mysterious envelope in hand. He was cautious as he walked up the slippery steps and across the front deck. The sleet made the wood slick, neutralizing the salt pellets he'd scattered earlier. The warmth that swirled out of the front door as he walked in was welcoming, carrying with it the smell of freshly brewed coffee. He shucked off his jacket and boots on the landing, while staring at the envelope from Las Vegas. He made his way into the kitchen, set the mail on the counter and poured a cup of coffee. Now what?

The name above the return address was familiar; Sam

Needles. Nate chummed around with her since the start of the school year almost four months earlier. Sam had abruptly left town in November, as her mother dragged her West. They went off to the shiny lights of Las Vegas, hoping for a fresh start for them both.

Blackie had met Sam a couple times when picking Nate up from the mall and school. He'd exchanged maybe 20 words with the girl. She seemed very nice, always showed him respect as Nate's dad. His son didn't seem to be 'in love' with her, rather it was more of a strong bond Nate and his two other buddies, Chopper and Casey, shared with the girl. The Gang of Four, inseparable. She was pretty, dressed nicely, probably wasn't ever on the honor roll but then neither was Nate.

"Screw it."

Blackie decided that seeing the contents was more important than honoring his son's privacy. He tore the envelope open. Inside was an airline folder containing a one-way ticket in the name of Nathan MacDonald from MSP to Las Vegas. It was dated next Friday, December 9th. 8 days out.

CHAPTER TWO
HIDE IT

Nate had been living with his Dad for 5 months, since the death of his mother. His parent's marriage ended 12 years earlier, with Carol getting custody and moving out of state. Her death at the hands of a drunk driver uprooted the boy, returning him to a home and father he barely remembered. The pain of the loss coupled with puberty's rampaging hormones lead to frictions between father and son. Raised voices led to long silences, the two males acting like two mules, each thinking the other needed to show some respect. Blackie being the adult, didn't always act like one.

He fiddled with the ticket, turning it over and over in his hands. No way the boy is getting this. Nope, un-unh. But then what? Only two options - toss it or hide it. Blackie couldn't bring himself to throw it away so instead he walked into the office where he spent so much of his time. He pulled an old family Bible off the shelf, thinking that's probably not going to be opened accidently. The envelope was tucked into the middle and the book returned to it's spot.

The clock read 9:30. Nate would be getting off the school

bus this afternoon at 3-ish, depending on how much the bus driver slowed down due to the weather and more importantly, if the kid even got on the damn bus. More and more, he skipped the trip, complaining about riding with the little kids. He prefered to stay in town and hang out with Chopper and Casey.

Those boys were all sort of outsiders. They didn't live on the streets, they had a home life. Their Moms had a place for them such as it was. Except for Nate, stuck with Dad. But none of them were the popular kids, they just got along, hung out. Three of a kind, four counting Sam, before she moved away to Sin City.

"Vegas, yeah that's so not happening."

He stared at the Bible there on the shelf and shook his head. This is gonna be trouble, he just knew it, trouble on steroids hiding in that holy book. A shiver ran thru him before he walked back to the kitchen.

The school bus didn't stop, didn't even slow down as it passed by almost 6 hours later. No Nate.

The boy did come home the next night, Friday night, on the bus. He went directly to his room. That weekend passed uneventfully, with minimal interaction between father and son.

Blackie felt guilty about the ticket, felt it's increasing

burden as each day passed. He held internal arguments about what was the right thing to do versus what was the smart thing. Being put in that position was awful, hiding that ticket from his son, but he was convinced 'It-Was-For-The-Best'...

Finally, due to simple inertia, leaving it hidden and unmentioned became the default path to take. He tried not to think about it, as if ignoring reality would somehow magically make it go away. An old ulcer flared up again, his guts churned with the stress. Angus couldn't sleep worth a damn anymore. Denial had it's cost.

##

"I dunno."

The three boys were huddled behind a convenience store, out of the wind on a cold Monday afternoon. Nate passed the cigarette to Chopper without taking a drag. Smoking was gross.

"What about Judy, or Don? They got wheels."

Chopper took a hit and shook his head. The wind swirled the smoke around his face when he said "Nah. I'll call Travis, he's got the pickup this week."

He passed the Winston over to Casey.

Nate was thinking 'We gotta find somewhere warm, this is

nasty' as he watched Chopper check his phone. He had skipped the bus, skipped half the school day again. School sucks, winter sucks... his train of thought was interrupted by an incoming call on his own phone. Sam!

"Hey girl, long time. 'Sup?"

"Nate! God, yes. Did ya get it, I thought you woulda called right away..."

"Get... what?"

He's thinking – a missed text? voice message... email?

"The ticket! I sent you a plane ticket! For like this Friday, my God, I thought you'd be so excited!"

Plane ticket. He thought hard, drawing a blank. Snail mail?

"I ain't got no mail, geez Sam, when did you send it? "

"We sent it like last Tuesday. Big envelope, made out to you. Awww, really? Shit, you gotta find it, ask your Dad, you gotta get to the airport Friday morning. That's 4 days!"

Ask Dad. Yeah. His anger began to rise. Motherf... His thoughts raced.

"So what's the deal? I come out and what? What about your Mom, is she cool?"

"Of course! She put up the money, bought the ticket. Mailed it. She knows things aren't working out for you there, says come out for a visit, call it a vacation, check it out. I don't know anybody out here, it'll be great! Oh you gotta come!"

Vacation. Sunshine. Nate glanced at Chopper as a gust blew a cold curtain of snow over the three boys, crowded into a corner shared with a reeking dumpster.

"Wow Sam, yeah, that sounds great! You're very convincing. Ha. I'll see if dear old Dad is holding out on me, figure out what's going on with the ticket thing. So this Friday huh? What time, where from?"

She filled in the details of his flight, got him up to speed with their situation out in Vegas and what things were like there. Her Mom had an extended lease on essentially a three-bedroom hotel suite, Sam is in a big-city school that kinda sucked. She was SO looking forward to his familiar face.

The boy wrapped up the call with a promise to contact her tomorrow night, to confirm possession of the ticket and a ride to the airport.

Vegas. Yeah Baby, going to Vegas! Being a one way trip didn't bother Nate in the least. It didn't even register with him, and why would it? It was getting him outa here!

Chopper came through, or rather Travis Harrison did, pulling up 15 minutes later in his Mom's truck. She didn't like driving on bad roads, so he had dropped her off at the hospital for her 2nd shift job. He grabbed the boys on his way home and they camped out in his basement that night. Nate told them all about his upcoming escape and how messed up it was if Blackie was gonna be a jerk. After several rounds of video games and a couple frozen pizzas, Nate and Chopper crashed out on the floor. Travis picked up his Mom, and in the morning, all three boys walked to school.

Nate didn't miss that bus ride home. Tuesday afternoon.

CHAPTER THREE
LYING DICKWEED

Supper at Casa MacDonald that evening was interesting. Blackie served his Hormel No Bean chili paired with hotdogs broiled in the oven. It was Nate's favorite meal. They were sitting at the table, the food dished up, ready to eat. The teenager had his opening prepared.

"Ever been to Vegas Dad?"

Blackie froze, eyes fixed on the motionless spoon suspended six inches from his open mouth.

Two beats passed, ah one anda two...

He jammed the spoon into his mouth then made waving motions with his hands, stalling for time. HOT HOT HOT!

Angus finally said "Ah yeah, with your Mom. Long time ago." He took several gulps of water, more stalling, wondering where this was headed.

"How was it?"

Blackie thought back to his honeymoon and the crazy vibe pulsing in the scene out there.

"It's an adult carnival. Lots of crap goes on, trouble... and well, hard partying. Why?"

"You remember my friend Sam. She moved there with her mom before Thanksgiving. I talked with her, she called me today."

Blackie was getting called now too, called out on his deception. They both know he can't lie for shit. He got up and acted like his bowl needed topping off with another spoon of chili. His back was towards Nate, his mind racing.

"Oh? And how, how are things for her, her and her Mom?"

"Great, yeah, they like it, no winter and stuff."

Here it comes. Anda a one and a two..

"They invited me out."

Crap. Shoulda seen this coming. Duh, kids have phones... yeah, she'd call about the freaking ticket. With his determined refusal to deal with the issue, Angus didn't think this out. He hadn't considered being challenged, had no ready response.

He took the offensive.

"Out to Vegas? In your dreams kid. That's no place for a 16-year-old on his own. C'mon, you think that's alright?"

"Not on my own, Sam's mom is there, an adult you know?? Sheesh!"

Nate was standing now, a fierce look on his face. Blackie leaned on the stove, head down, shoulders slumped. Silent

Nate thought- he's gonna do it, is going to fess up, yeah, obvious guilt-city. His Dad raised his eyes to the ceiling and then turned to look at his son.

"I can think of a million reasons why that's just dumb." His voice was low, his tone calm. "You're tanking in school. You don't come home two nights out of the week. You're kind of a smartass to me. And it's trouble Nate. Too young, another year, get your grades up..." The words blurred together to the boy, all he heard was a droning adult voice, no no no...

The boy was livid. "Geez, chill. Vacation, a visit ya know. It aint like I'd be moving out there or nothing!" all the while thinking 'who's being a lying dickweed now huh?'

Blackie knew it was a one way ticket. He could spring for a return flight, set a deadline, not let it be an open-ended deal. He could. Try to work out some arrangement. This was his last chance to quit being a hard ass. But that was quickly discarded.

He was convinced the boy wouldn't come back. There wasn't much exciting about Podunk MN, especially after the bright lights. Besides, that would be admitting to his deception.

That would suck.

It's in the boy's best interest he decided. Gonna go with that.

"Let's talk about a vacation AFTER you buckle down and do some work in school. You got your whole life to earn money, take trips, do adult stuff but that's after school. First things first, whadda say?"

Nate rose up and looked Blackie right in the eye.

"Then what I say is, got any mail for me Dad?"

He couldn't maintain eye contact with his son. He turned and walked out of the kitchen after tossing out a single word reply. "No!"

Blackie felt like a jerk but kept telling himself, for the boy's own good, too young, harrumph. He went downstairs to flop into his LazyBoy, to zone out in front to the tube. Nate stomped out of the kitchen and went to his room. They easily, silently avoided each other the rest of that night.

Sam got a profanity filled call around 10PM. Nate replayed the conversation for her, with pointed negative aspersions on his father's intellect, moral turpitude and parenting skills. The girl was appalled at Blackie's actions, outright lying to Nate like that, destroying her plans for them to get together.

Nate assured her he'd find a way, somehow, to make it out there. His Dad thought he'd won, he'd got his way. But the boy was resolute, there just had to be some way for him to get to Vegas and he'd find it. He'd show Dad, this wasn't over, he wasn't giving up.

Nate left for school Wednesday morning. Blackie saw him back home that afternoon. Unknown to his Dad, the boy had settled on a rudimentary plan, and had begun preparations to execute it. Nate maintained a neutral, albeit it silent attitude.

Thursday started out the same. They passed in the hallway and kitchen wordlessly, the boy doing his laundry (oddly without being prompted). Blackie worked in his office, made supper, ate alone. He conked out in front of the big screen as the Wild throttled the Blackhawks, leaving his son to his own devices upstairs. He awoke and went up to bed, stopping in the bathroom before falling into a deep sleep in his king-sized bed. Snow began lightly falling outside. It was one AM Friday morning.

CHAPTER FOUR
WHOA

Not needing an alarm clock is a beautiful thing. For the working man, it's what differentiates the weekend. A respite, to sleep in for a change. Angus supported himself with random freelance writing jobs, a little bit of handy man/small engine stuff and a family trust fund. But mostly the trust fund. For him, sleeping in was the norm, not the exception.

That Friday morning, he lay in bed and shook off the effects of a heavy slumber. He noticed the faint traces of light in his bedroom window. Seven-thirtyish he estimated, confirmed by the bedside clock.

He shuffled to the bathroom, did his morning routine and got dressed. The house was silent. On his way to the kitchen, he rapped on Nate's door in passing.

"Yo. Breakfast?"

No response. That could mean F U Dad or he wasn't awake yet. Whatever. Blackie started assembling a man's meal.

Meat, potatoes, cheese, nom nom... and coffee. Coffee first. He started the pot brewing and began to gather the ingredients; Black Label bacon, russets, onions, and cheese. With the first burner turned up on the stovetop, he added a non-stick skillet with a dash of peanut oil and pepper flakes. As that got hot, potatoes were shredded and tossed in. A second pan received the yummy bacon.

Blackie finally poured himself a cup of coffee. He moved over to a stool by the east window while waiting for the hash browns to get crisper before adding the onion. Satisfied that the food was on track, he took a glance out the window overlooking the highway and took his first sip.

It didn't register right away. The Honda. His Honda. In the ditch. Blackie had the dumbest thought, 'That's not where I left it.' The tracks clearly showed an exit from the shed but then they stopped and turned too quickly, sliding down and off the driveway. It ended up nose first into the snow packed ditch.

Footprints led back to the shed.

Then he noticed a second pair of tracks. They too exited the shed, but these went far enough back to make the turn, to get down the driveway. And onto Highway 63. He shifted over to get a better view of the shed.

Overhead door open. Two sets of car tracks, one ending in the ditch, the other merging onto the southbound lane, headed toward town. Two empty stalls in the shed. The Honda in the ditch, the Cutlass AWOL. And then it hit him.

He stole a car, MY car. TWO of my cars! And went to Vegas. He couldn't help but laugh. The kid stole my freaking car, went to freaking Vegas. Cause it's Friday after all. Departure Day. He was all booked and shit.

Blackie finished his manly breakfast and ate at the dining room table. By the depth of the snow in the tire tracks and the rate it continued to fall, he knew the boy had left hours earlier. He tried to recall the extent of Nate's driving experience. Not very damn much. A couple of sessions behind the wheel of the F150, once or twice in the Cutlass. Once in a mall parking lot, a little on the highway. Nothing recent... was that his choice or mine? He didn't recall the kid pestering him to go out driving, which upon reflection, seemed uncharacteristic of a teenager. Doesn't matter. The kid is gone, getting some driving in now. Stole my car, went to Vegas.

He cleaned the kitchen and geared up to go outside. Snow boots, parka, hat and gloves were needed for this extended outing. His old truck reluctantly fired up and idled as he scraped the windows and tracked down the log chain he'd need. A trek down into the ditch followed by flopping to his knees to eyeball the Civic's plight was reassuring, no damage, the undercarriage clear, a convenient spot to easily attach the hook was located. He got the chain on, then stood and brushed off his jeans.

The snow was deep along the driver's door when he opened it. A quick check of tranny was followed by a shift into neutral, which made the car settle another foot into the ditch. He got out and walked the chain back uphill to a level spot. Blackie climbed into the pickup and maneuvered it into position. A quick exit to connect to the hitch and he was back inside. It took a couple of attempts, finally requiring 4WD LOW to pull the small car backwards up to the driveway.

The Honda fired up right away (keys conveniently left in the ignition, gee thanks Nate) and Blackie took another 15 minutes or so to let it idle, while he put the pickup into the stall vacated so recently by the Oldsmobile. After both vehicles were situated, Angus closed up the shed and returned to the house. Stole my car, that's a hoot.

It was clear he'd be getting a call soon. The kid won't get far in this snow, 'umpossible'. Any minute now.

Then out of the blue it occurred to him; the outcome might be worse, much worse than another gentle slide into a ditch somewhere. It could involve other vehicles. Nate or someone else could get hurt. Stole my car, went to Vegas wasn't so damn funny anymore.

With things back in order outdoors, Blackie realized he had some calls to make. And maybe, hopefully one to receive. It occurred to him that he hadn't even tried to call Nate yet. Duh...

He punched the speed dial. One ring and it rolled to voice mail. That caught him off guard, he wasn't prepared to leave a message, was flustered at first.

"Ah Nate, this is Dad. Very funny, ha ha. Well really, I ah, I see you're gone and I, well I just wanna say come home. Be careful, pull over, lets talk about things, just ah, well shit Nate. Come home!"

He looked at the phone for a minute after he hung up and then stuffed it in his pocket. He needed to start a list of who else to contact. He ticked them off in his head as he went back to the kitchen; Chopper, Casey, what was that other kid's name... Larry, Gimpy, goofball maybe not goofball... And the cops. Blackie poured another cup of coffee and sat down with paper and pencil. Cops last.

Chopper didn't answer, and Blackie didn't leave a message. Casey did answer. Obviously, school wasn't the chosen option for him that day, he responded with a sleep filled voice.

"Hey Casey, this is Nate's Dad, Angus."

"Uh, yeah?"

"I, ah, I don't think Nate went to school today... Have you heard from him, maybe know what his plans might be?"

"Um, Nate, no, no, I haven't talked to him. Why?"

Angus counted to three. "Really Casey, no idea, none?"

"No sir."

"Dude, my fricking car is gone, another one's in the ditch. Nate split. What do you know about that?"

"Nate took your car?... Um, yeah. I guess I do remember he said something about taking off. Ah, he said he was thinking about, ah, Florida. Wow."

"Yeah, wow. Florida. OK. Thanks, you've been very helpful. If you hear from him, let me know, OK?"

"Um, sure Mr. Mac. I'll let you know first thing."

Blackie hung up. Florida, I'm sure. Wrong direction dummy. He took another sip of coffee. Stole my car. Vegas. Like the kid said, Wow. He stared out the window at the tracks in the ditch, examining his options. Stole my car means call and report a stolen car. He finished the cup of coffee and walked into his office to get a phone book.

"Olmsted County Sheriff, how may I direct your call?"

"Yeah, I'd like to report a stolen car."

"Name and address?"

"Angus MacDonald, 2600 Hwy 63N, Roch, 906."

"Phone number?"

"It's on your display."

"Description of the stolen vehicle?"

Angus gave some details, described the vehicle and the

time. The dispatcher said they'd issue an APB alerting the authorities to the situation. After a few more questions, when it was revealed that the supposed thief was a family member, the dispatcher said; "This isn't really a stolen vehicle, is it Mr. MacDonald?"

"Well, my car is gone, without my permission, taken by an unlicensed driver. I'd like the police or sheriff or highway patrol to assist me in getting it back."

"Sir, when a family member is involved, it doesn't rise to the level of 'Stolen Vehicle' but I will send out a request for law enforcement to be on the lookout for a Black 98 Cutlass with the license of BAT 262. I have your contact info, we'll call you with any news."

"Ah, the kid is gone, what about a missing person report?"

"There has to be a 24-hour absence before we'll open one sir. That would be tomorrow. Anything else for me today?"

That was all Blackie was going to get from that call, so he

said, "Let me know, thanks." and hung up.

Stole my car. Went to Vegas. Whoa.

CHAPTER FIVE
NO MAIL, NO CUTLASS

The northern Iowa rest area ROCKED. The perfect distance from home for a pit stop. Get out and stretch the legs, go in to pee, get a drink from the fountain. He checked out his location on a large wall-mounted map of Iowa.

It was 9 AM. He'd been on the road for four hours, a felon for the same length of time. He had turned off his cell phone before leaving, going silent, untraceable he hoped. Driving was kinda easy; he laughed. Easier in this car anyway. What was he thinking, taking that stupid stick-shift Honda? He'd just about pissed his pants when he rode the Civic into the snow filled ditch.

Dad's gonna be steamed. He laughed, a little. It was kinda shitty grabbing the car, TWO cars, and leaving without a word.

But Sam confirmed she'd mailed the ticket. Blackie really had it coming, acting all 'What, mail? Why no, no mail for you son' -what a dick. No mail, no Cutlass Dad.

Nate stepped outside and took a lap around the building, noticed the wind picking up. A few snowflakes danced past the overhead lights. He figured to get thru Des Moines, stop for gas and breakfast on the West side, get some miles racked up. Vegas wasn't coming to him.

He got back behind the wheel. It still felt weird, driving. He took a couple minutes to get situated. A glance in the back showed his inventory of Mountain Dew, chocolate doughnuts, a couple Red Bulls. Nate opened a Dew and took a long pull.

"Lets do this. One more time!"

He fiddled with the radio and found a classic rock station. AC/DC would be his traveling companions for the next 4 minutes. Adjusting the seat, checking the mirrors, he slid the car into reverse, slowly easing backwards into the access road. Turning forwards, he slid into drive and then braked, roughly

The windshield was slowly filling with large fat snowflakes. He couldn't spot the wiper controls for several moments, but finally located it and cleared the glass. A car behind him honked, which made him flinch.

His tires spun as he nervously goosed the accelerator, finally easing the Cutlass to the side, straddling a couple of parking spaces. The other car pulled around, the driver slowing to stare at Nate, shaking his head and expressing unkind thoughts. Nate took several deep breaths and then flipped the radio off. Maybe just driving, doing the pedal, wheel, mirrors thing is enough to concentrate on. To start with anyway, until this snow quits, and the sun comes out. It'll warm up, be much nicer. Then we'll rock out.

He guided the car slowly out of the rest area, back onto I 35 southbound, heading for a hookup with I 80 going West. 65 seemed awful fast with the snow starting to stick to the roadway. He slowed to 60 and gripped the wheel tightly. Vegas Baby. For the first time since Mom died, he was looking forward to something. A new start in a new place. Vegas Baby. Vegas and Sam. The wipers beat out a rhythm as he hunched over the wheel, staring into the worsening conditions.

##

Blackie paced back and forth between his kitchen and the office, convinced his phone would ring any second now and Nate's adventure would be over. It just had to, the odds were stacked against him, weather and cops gonna tag team the mad dash. Any second now.

But his phone didn't ring. He thought of getting online and searching 'runaway kids from the Midwest' but realized that would be ill-advised for his mental state. Thinking of advice, who does he know that he could bounce some questions off?

"Dave, my man. Angus here. Long time no talk to bud!"

"Blackie! Hey, it HAS been a long time. How the hell are you?"

Dave was a college roomie from back in the day, a computer guy that worked at a cable company. Blackie's go-to nerd resource.

"Well, I'd be better if Nate didn't just steal my car and take off for parts unknown."

A pause. "WUT! Stole your car? Wow, Sorry to hear that. Did you guys have a blowup or something, did ya see it coming?"

"Na. Teen angst, I suppose. A girl from school moved out to Vegas, wanted Nate to come out and live it up I guess. I let him know that wasn't happening and we kind of dropped it. No big argument or nothing... The girl did send him a plane ticket, one way, that I, well I kind of intercepted. He asked if he'd gotten any mail, the little shit, trying to trap me."

"Ruh Roh. And you said...?"

"Well, I didn't respond 100% truthfully, so I guess he quickly realized his old man was a lying piece of crap... and was pretty pissed about it. It seemed like the right approach at the time."

"And now?"

"Now, not so much. I didn't know he'd take my car and run."

"That's brutal man. How can I help?"

"I'm thinking he has his phone. Not answering it, or not answering my calls anyway. I'm wondering if there's a way to pinpoint his location some way, using the phone?"

"Yeah, probably. If he disabled the locate function that 911 uses, and that a lot of apps use, which he's smart enough to know about, then the only opportunity to zero in on him is if he turns it back on, he picks up or makes a call. Verizon could tell what cell tower was involved, which would narrow it down to a couple of miles. You pay the bill, right, in your name?"

"Yeah."

"So call them, get a trace or something going."

Dave asked what he'd done so far, how involved is law enforcement? Blackie outlined it was NOT classified as a stolen vehicle so probably no guns drawn.

Stating that, no guns drawn, made him suddenly a little queasy. Dave started explaining the technology involved in cell phones, distracting him. Blackie kept repeating that the kid can't drive, the weather wasn't getting better, he'd be getting a call after the Cutlass AND the boy were found in a ditch, really any minute now. He wrapped up the conversation with a promise to keep Dave up to date.

He poured himself another cup of coffee and settled into his chair at the kitchen table, paper and sharpie already in place.

What needs to be done next to help get Nate back? He started a list.

Call Verizon, see about the trace.

Try to contact Sam? Yeah, she may be hard to track down and I don't know if she'd tell me if she knew anything. He wondered about waiting to call Sam, putting that confrontation off a bit. Maybe give it a day to get sorted out.

With the embarrassingly short, single item list taunting him, he picked up his phone.

Verizon gave Blackie the runaround, for a time anyway. Verify this, verify that, my name is ON the account OK and my credit card PAYS the balance each and every month, que pasa? So yes, he was entitled to all the access and reporting available. This wasn't an unusual situation apparently and they had a protocol in place. He got hooked up, got the 'call Angus if the number hits' flag in place, which was the goal. The kid was running silent and deep. Blackie sent up another quick plea for a safe resolution to the Lord above and thanked the Verizon rep. He hung up and returned to pacing, trying to think of another item for the to-do list.

CHAPTER SIX
SISTERS

This driving stuff gets old. Nate was tired. He was up most of last night, waiting for the house to quiet down, for Dad to fall asleep. Then the rush of the getaway amped him up to begin the journey. But after 10 plus hours of staring out the windshield, trying to peer thru the snow-blotted blur and with a muscle-numbing death grip on the steering wheel, his whole body ached. Not to mention crashing off a couple energy drinks.

A sign announced a truck stop ahead. Omaha Nebraska. He managed to stay alert to the exit, negotiating the off ramp and turning into the brightly lit oasis. 2:30, not yet dark. Driving around to the rear, he spotted a relatively isolated corner. He awkwardly backed in and turned off the ignition. Exhaustion overpowered his growing hunger. Sliding down into the seat and unbuckling the belt, he quickly fell asleep.

##

Elsie Carter got off at the Broadmoor Village office with all the other high school kids. Her sister was already waiting by the doorway; the elementary bus arrived first.

"Hey Lou!" The sisters exchanged smiles. "Hey Els! How'd

you do on that test?"

    They started across the lot to the third set of apartment buildings, chattering away about the school day, not noticing the cluster of people or the reflections of flashing lights around the corner. Finally, seeing the commotion, Elsie stopped, and grabbed Lou's hand. The older girl spotted a couple of familiar faces, neighbors, suddenly turning towards the two girls and raising their hands to point as they spoke with police. Elsie's stomach lurched.

    A policewoman swiftly crossed the lot towards the girls, coming from their building, D. The entryway passage was filled with EMT personnel. 2 cop cars and an ambulance had their lights flashing outside the building.

    "Elsie and Louise Carter? I'm Officer Nelson, please come with me." The uniformed adult took Lou's other wrist and started to pull her over to a nearby cop car.

    Elsie tugged back, screaming "No! What are you doing? Let go of my sister!" The younger girl was jerked one way, then another. She began to scream.

    Another woman joined them in the parking lot. She squatted down to Lou's eye level and put her hands on the girl's shoulders. She identified herself, said she was with Social Services.

"Girls, we'd like to talk with you just for a minute, away from all these people. Over here please, follow Officer Nelson."

Elsie was tense, the crowd, the lights. "Where's Mom? I don't wanna go with you, where's Mom?" The parking lot was full of people milling around.

The female officer let go of Lou's arm as she turned to the older girl, getting in her face. Elsie squeezed her eyes shut. Her mind was racing, 'What to DO?' She avoided thinking of what might have happened with Mom although she knew. Another OD, it had to be.

BANG! The outside door of the apartment building blasted open as a gurney crashed thru it. Both women turned towards the sound, rising to their feet. All the onlookers focused on the cart with the covered form on top.

Elsie realized this was their moment! She grabbed Lou by the wrist again and they took off, running East thru the crowded lots. They wove around parked cars, thru the maze of buildings, and left any pursuit far behind.

##

The sisters huddled together in a Burger King booth, nursing a value fries bought with the change they were able to scrape together from their backpacks. It wasn't enough, they were still hungry. The wall mounted TV had a muted news channel on, it was 7:30PM. The window looked out at the ER entrance across the street where Mom had arrived three hours earlier, in the ambulance. Again. The older girl knew what came next. Detox and rehab for Mom. Foster home for them.

Not this time. Sooner or later social services won't let the cycle repeat, won't let their mother get her girls back when she's released. The sisters could easily end up separated, Elsie had heard things in the handful of foster homes they'd had to endure before. Brothers and sisters got split up all the time.

"C'mon Lou, Quit it. Stop acting like a baby."

Lou punched her sister's arm. "I'm not a baby! But but... Mom.." trailing off into sobs again. Elsie wrapped her arm around the 11-year-old.

We need a plan. Not gonna walk over there and let them take us away! Not again- THINK!

Mom has a sister, out West somewhere. We only met her once, but she was cool. Aunt... Traci. Elsie remembered Traci seemed upset to see how Mom was doing, how we were living. She felt bad, took us out to eat, gave Mom some money. That was last summer. Utah, yeah, Utah. Spanish something, spoon, knife. I bet a map would show it. Elsie started feeling better with the beginnings of a plan. Or at least a destination. But Utah was a long way from this fast food joint.

Lou stopped crying, pulled away and sat up straight, getting composed. "Want the last fry?"

"No Sis, you go ahead. I got an idea how this can turn out different. Better maybe. Hopefully."

She pulled Lou close, whispering her daring decision.

Lou sat back, brow furrowed, finally nodding her head yes.

"I'm sick of being in those horrible homes. Mom can't take care of us anymore. But you can, you'll take care of us won't you?"

Elsie assured her she could and would.

"OK. I'm in. Now what?"

Elsie looked out the other side of the building, towards the Interstate.

"That's what. Over there"

##

Nate's bladder woke him. He groggily re-oriented himself, then sat up and looked around. The windows were covered in frost. He couldn't detect any activity around the car so he put the keys in his pocket and got out. The main truck stop complex was 100 yards away, brightly lit. As he headed to it, traffic was steady on I-80 to his left.

The boy stepped inside and shook off the chill. Of immediate interest, a sign directed him to the rest rooms. After relieving himself (the pause that refreshes as Dad said) he washed up. The mirror showed a disheveled 16 year old, red eyed, with wild dirty blonde hair. The boy wet his hands in the sink, then plastered down the strands, running his fingers through the stringy locks in a poor imitation of a comb. He made a mental note to get a toothbrush and toothpaste after breakfast and with one last look, decided he was mostly presentable enough to go and order some food.

The restaurant was in the front, past a large aisle full of snack and impulse items. He noticed a clock exiting the restroom; 7 PM. Friday night. Four and a half hours of sleep. Not bad, better after eating.

Nate decided on a booth rather than a stool at the counter

and slid into the first open one on the right. He grabbed a menu then mentally counted his remaining money; after filling up with gas yet again and a minimal breakfast, he'd have around $120 left. Guessing (hoping) that three more tanks of gas would get him to Vegas, he'd be cutting it real close.

A pretty waitress that looked just a couple of years older than Nate stopped at his booth and graced him with a big smile. Her name tag read 'BETTY'.

"Hey Hon, you ready to order?"

"Yes. Pancakes. And, orange juice. Please."

She gave him the once over after memorizing the two-item order, thinking 'kinda cute but just a kid.' Betty turned and left, giving Nate an opportunity to watch her backside as she headed to the kitchen. His eyes roamed the rest of the area and took note of the other customers. Truckers seemed to prefer the stools, while couples generally sat at booths. His booth was the only one with a sole occupant. The noise level slowly decreased as more people finished their meals and left. Supper time was over.

A large plate of fluffy pancakes soon appeared in front of him, along with three kinds of syrup. Betty set down a 16 ounce glass of awesome looking orange juice and asked if he needed anything else. No, he was good. Good and hungry. Slathering on the butter and drowning the pancakes with maple, blueberry AND pecan goodness, Nate dug in.

Very filling. He'd been focused on stuffing his face as he worked through the stack. Betty stopped by to ask how everything was; oh it was just fine. Heavenly in fact. She brought him a refill of OJ, which he polished off after the pancakes were gone. Yes, breakfast was a good idea, and the pancakes were cheap enough, and filling enough, that he can probably skip eating until breakfast tomorrow. Fed for 12, maybe 14 hours if he could stay behind the wheel that long. Plus gas and bathroom breaks. He wondered how far he could get in another 12 hours; would that get him all the way there? He really had no idea of the distance involved, was in the middle of finding out.

He left $1.50 tip on the table, grabbed the check and started towards the register.

There was some kind of ruckus going on; the cashier was speaking harshly to a girl. The overweight woman came out from behind the register and got a tight grip on the younger girl. Then a second girl, about Nate's age, arrived.

Suddenly a scream of pain erupted from the cashier, quickly followed by the first girl breaking free and taking off outside . The second one had some words then pushed her way past and flew out the doors too. A string of profanity flew as the limping clerk headed out in weak pursuit. Nate chuckled as he made his way up front, entertained by the unexpected drama in the truck stop.

CHAPTER SEVEN
SHE'S DEAD!

Lou huddled behind the end car in the front row of the parking lot, scared out of her wits. Suddenly, the truckstop door flew open and Elsie exploded onto the sidewalk, running like crazy.

"Over here!" Lou called.

The other girl changed directions and yanked her younger sister by the arm as she raced past. Together they headed around to the rear of the building, where the lighting was a little more scattered. Edging between two idling trucks, the girls remained silent as they moved steadily alongside the red and yellow lit trailers. Finally, Elsie stopped and turned to Lou, who burst into tears as she wrapped her arms around her older sister.

"I didn't know what to DO when that lady yelled at me!"

"You did fine honey. Look, we both made it out. It's OK, you're OK. We both are!"

Elsie and Lou stayed in their embrace for several more moments, as the 11-year-old gradually regained her composure.

Elsie said "What'd you get?"

Lou unzipped her parka.

"Some chips that kinda got crushed in our hug. A Hershey bar and.." she reached deeper into the jacket and pulled out the final item.

"A bag of cashews. What'd you get?"

"Away from the clerk is all. Wish I'd got a water or something, that stuffs gonna make us thirsty!"

Elsie swiveled her head from side to side, assessing their situation and soon decided on a course of action. Holding hands, the sisters headed across the parking lot and past several rows of trucks, The girls went West, taking the shoulder of the frontage road and walking past some darkened industrial buildings.

Elsie thought there might be a park, she remembered seeing a sign. They needed to figure out their next move, lay low and gather their thoughts after that narrow escape.

##

Nate watched as the heavy-set cashier returned to her register empty-handed. Wheezing, she collapsed on a stool and massaged her left foot.

"What was all that?" he asked.

"Damn shoplifters! Two of them! I caught the little one red handed, had her by the arm. Then the bigger girl stomped on my toe, the bitch! Damn that hurts!"

"Sorry kid, excuse my cussing."

Nate placed the ticket on the counter and pulled his wad of money from his front jeans pocket. Counting out five single dollar bills, he slid them towards the still out of breath woman. He waited for his nickel change, then went outside. Pausing, he looked around for anyone fleeing the scene of the crime. Nada. With a shrug, he headed towards his car.

He didn't catch a good look at the first girl, saw even less of the other one. It all happened so quickly. Nate had never really gotten into shoplifting. Several of his friends did though, one, Chopper, REALLY got proficient at it. The fear of getting caught and the resulting embarrassment is what kept Nate on the straight and narrow. At least concerning shoplifting; grand theft auto is way different. He chuckled at the thought as he reached the car. He slipped behind the wheel and started it up. Daylight was gone, no moon visible thru the overcast skies. A long winter night had begun.

Nate slowly rolled through the rear of the lot, past the rows of idling trucks with assorted trailers. He turned and pulled up to the gas pumps, for his second fill-up. The first one outside

Des Moines didn't go so well; he was on the wrong side of the pump for the gas cap and fumbled around trying to get the damn access door to open. Another driver watched his antics and took pity on the boy, pointed out where the release button was located. This time he knew what had to be done and did it.

He returned to the building, to the same cashier, and forked over $35 out of his dwindling stash. He replayed the episode of the two girls doing a number on the fat unpleasant woman and was unable to keep a smirk off his face as she thanked him. Nate returned to the car and settled in for another long stretch behind the wheel, refreshed and refueled.

Leaving, he pulled up to the stop sign on the service road with the nose of the Oldsmobile actually poking into the street. As he looked both ways, he spotted two figures walking along the shoulder to his right, about ¼ mile away. If he hadn't looked at that precise instant, as the girls walked into the illuminating cone thrown by a nearby streetlight, he would have missed them. That's gotta be those two, he thought. Impulsively, he flipped on his blinker and slowly rounded the corner.

Elsie immediately sensed the approaching car. She swept her eyes across their surroundings, looking for cover. Spotting a fence alongside a darkened plumbing shop, she jerked her sister's arm, dragging her into the parking lot. They scrambled to maneuver between a dumpster and some beatup van. Hunkered down and terrified, they both waited to see what the driver would do, hoping he'd roll on past.

Elsie muttered "Shit shit shit!" as the car pulled to a stop, blocking the driveway. She looked for another exit, tracing the chain link fence around the perimeter. No! She had got them trapped here, with no way out! What a FOOL!

The car just sat there, idling ominously. Lou held her older sister tight, face buried in Elsie's jacket, trembling with fear. Then the driver rolled down a passenger-side window.

After a long pause, a voice calls out.

"Hey! You guys alright?"

A boy's voice.

Elsie didn't know what to think. It wasn't an adult, wasn't the fat lady. Could she trust that voice? Her uncertainty kept her quiet. Lou looked at her, panic in her eyes.

"I was in the truck stop and saw you go tearing out the door." Nate paused. Both girls held their breath. A siren started wailing in the distance.

"The cashier fell chasing you."

Another dramatic pause.

"Heart attack. They said.. she's DEAD!"

Elsie gasped loudly, couldn't catch her breath. They'd call it murder! She KILLED that poor fat old lady. Tears welled up in her eyes.

Then she heard Nate's soft laughter.

The sorrow evaporated instantly, replaced by a hot anger.

"You think that's FUNNY? Jeez, I believed you! What an asshole!"

She jumped up and marched rapidly towards the car. The boy quit laughing as she stuck her head in the open window and punched his arm, hard.

"Hey. Don't take it out on me, Killer!"

Nate started laughing again. Elsie shook her head and then she started laughing too. Lou came up to the car and looked at them both like they were nuts.

"What's so funny? I don't get it."

Elsie and Nate laughed even louder.

The laughter gradually died out. Nate got out and walked around to meet the girls. He offered his hand to Elsie, taking in her features, liking what he saw.

"I'm Nathan MacDonald. Nate. Pleased to meet you!"

Elsie shook his hand, replying,

"I'm Elsie and this is my sister, Lou."

Turning towards the younger girl, he shook her hand.

"Hey Lou, nice to meet 'choo too!" He noticed that Elsie didn't volunteer a last name.

"Are you guys going far? On foot and all..?"

He glanced around, not seeing anything that would be a likely destination for these two girls at that time of day. Or any time of day.

Elise glanced at Lou with frown, an unspoken warning to keep quiet. She answered his question with one of her own.

"Where YOU going Nate?"

He quickly replied. "Las Vegas."

"What's in Las Vegas?"

"A friend just moved out there, wants me to join her."

"Her?" A pause, then she continued "A girlfriend?"

Nate blushed. "A friend that's a girl."

His turn to put it back on Elsie, "You still haven't said where you're going."

"West, we're heading West too. Somewhere away from here."

"Are you walking there? West I mean."

The sisters glanced at each other, didn't reply.

Nate was quiet for a minute, then he blurted out – "My trip has been kinda boring. It'd sure be nice to have some company."

A look at Lou, before he focused on Elsie, hoping she's say yes. He realized he had to make it a real invitation. "Can I offer you two a ride?"

Elsie pondered the situation; they had to get out of town but didn't have wheels. Or money. Which made traveling pretty challenging. The boy seemed nice enough; she wasn't getting any 'danger' vibes off him and her intuition was almost always reliable. She reached out to shake Nate's hand again, smiling broadly.

"We'll take you up on your kind offer sir and we thank you. Very much!"

Lou had a quizzical expression on her face, like this is some formal ritual she wasn't aware of. However, she understood their predicament as clearly as Elsie did and also felt this boy was someone they could trust. Besides, the girls had him outnumbered.

She shook Nate's hand too, then opened the back door to climb in, throwing her backpack across the seat. Nate opened the front passenger door for the older girl, then got back behind the wheel.

"Buckle up ladies!" which they did.

The freshly blended trio began a new, shared stage of their respective journeys. They drove back past the truck stop (Elsie scrunching down in the passenger seat) and got going on Westbound 80.

The boy fiddled with the radio until another car's horn brought his attention back to driving. Elsie took over as DJ, selecting a pop station to provide their sound track on that cold night in Eastern Nebraska.

Driving with companions was much better than driving solo. Female companions were even better. Nate smiled at that thought and turned to Elsie riding shotgun.

"So, shoplifter huh?"

Her brow furrowed, cheeks flushed. "I've NEVER done that before! Ever! Lou will tell ya. I thought we'd get something to eat, scope out the scene, see how we were going to get a ride. And ya know what, ha ha, it worked! Here we are, on the road!" She let out a whoop. Nate laughed and threw out a "Hoo Rah!" Lou added a "Yippee!" from the backseat. It was Elsie's turn to dig at Nate a little.

"Pretty decent car for such a newbie driver like yourself."

"What 'choo talking 'bout Newbie? Huh!" He turned towards her while saying this and the girl squealed a little as a tire hit the rumble strips along the shoulder. He then over-corrected, sending them over the centerline. Luckily the left lane was unoccupied.

"Eyes on the road!"

"Yes ma'am."

With a more focused driver, the threesome settled in.

CHAPTER EIGHT
RUNAWAY EXPRESS

Lou had fallen asleep in the back. Nate and Elsie were quietly talking back and forth, lowering the radio volume to not disturb the younger girl's rest. Elsie heard all about the boy's departure from home. A few leading questions drew the story out of him, like he was looking for someone to tell it to. A trickle of words turned into a gusher as he outlined his mother's death, moving in with a father he didn't know, unhappiness at school. He described a home life that to Elsie sounded pretty desirable, and then spoke of his father's betrayal and the resulting escape.

He spoke at length, finally winding down as his narrative came to their chance meeting. She was on the lookout for and didn't find any evidence of any feelings of 'love' between the girl in Vegas and this boy beside her. That made her feel much better about HER impulsive decision to get in the car with him, to tie her and her sister's fate to his.

The dashboard clock hit midnight, so it became Saturday now. It dropped below 10 degrees outside but the car was toasty warm. Nate bumped up the temperature an hour earlier, at the 'woe is me, school is hard' stage of his narrative. The two teens had been silent for 15 miles or so.

Elsie leaned back against the headrest, then reclined her seat to a more comfortable position. She was bothered by something he'd said, something important. A memory of some kind. She tried to recall what it was, what he said that triggered the feeling, but it wouldn't come into focus. Maybe a catnap would help. Her eyelids got heavier inside the overheated vehicle. Soon, she was lightly snoring.

Nate glanced at her profile, smiling slightly at the way she held her mouth open. He recalled Lou's features; yup, they were certainly sisters, the resemblance was obvious.

He realized he had pretty much spilled his guts to this virtual stranger, but he felt better for doing so. She knew a LOT about him now; he knew next to nothing about them. That would change, it would be his turn to ask the questions about how the two girls ended up at that particular 'Travelers Plaza' at that instant in time. Was it a cosmic fluke that their paths crossed? Was it destiny? Whatever the mechanism, things could have turned out much worse.

By the driver's estimate, they'll need to stop for gas again in a couple hours. He began to decide on which upcoming town or intersection would be the one. He mentally tallied his cash on hand minus food for three of them instead of just himself. Minus gas. He didn't think it would be enough. Maybe he'd skip eating. Drive a little slower to improve his mileage. He wondered if the girls had any money. He actually wondered about a LOT of things concerning these two. The miles and hours rolled by.

##

Blackie's Friday night wasn't much different than the rest of that day. He waited for news, waited for the call that didn't come. Worried about Nate. The list did have one additional entry; he called the bank and found out the kid left with just under $180, assuming the savings account was his entire funding source. He tried to remember how full the tank was in the Cutlass but really had no idea. So he had added one line to his list and now crossed it off.

Supper consisted of left overs, dessert was a six pack.

He flopped in the recliner and watched the early late news.

As expected, they didn't lead with any reports of runaways or stolen vehicles, but he couldn't really recall what the content was. His brain was cycling thru a zillion things; what-ifs, likely (and increasingly unlikely) scenarios that would explain the lack of news. Could Nate really be lucky enough, or a good enough driver, or have his own guardian angel that could keep him STILL on the road? All day and no word. Was that good or bad?

He fell into a restless sleep, the phone at his side still silent.

##

Nate was getting tired, really tired. The gas gauge was dipping towards the final quarter tank. Pit stop for fuel and sleep for him. Elsie had been keeping him company for a couple of hours following a little nap. It had been a long day for all of them. He asked Lou to look at the atlas, see what options were coming up soon, turned on the dome light for her.

"We're taking a break, Els. Gas and sleep." He yawned

She nodded and smiled at Nate, then stretched out her arms, turning to look out her side window. Their day had started a long time ago, filled with a lot of stress and drama. Her nap wasn't nearly long enough. She reached back and grabbed her sister's leg. "What does the navigator say?"

Lou had been dreaming, about their trip and about their Aunt. The dream was still fresh in her thoughts as she processed a response.

"Ogallala Nebraska coming up soon, 30 miles or so. There's a rest area, probably truck stops."

"Are we missing any scenery driver?"

Nate laughed.

"White and dirty white. Flat as a pancake."

She groaned when he mentioned food. Her stomach started growling, which triggered another round of giggling by both.

"Are you guys hungry? When did you last eat?"

Elsie looked out the front, hesitating before answering.

"This morning. No wait, yesterday. We had breakfast at school."

He decided to pry a little. It was her turn to give out some info.

"School huh. Back in Omaha huh? Going to school, you and your sister, and living with.."

She looked at Nate, "We were living with our Mom and going to school. And now we're not."

He saw the pain on her face.

"You're not... because...."

"We lost our Mom too, in a way. She was sick, got taken

away. They wanted to take us too. But"… her voice trailed off. Lou let out a quiet sob in the back. Elsie raised her face defiantly. Nope, not gonna start crying, that's behind us.

"Well, you're a runaway! Car thief too, you said so. Well Lou and I are runaways, just the same! We're all running away, riding in this runaway express."

She took a quick glance to check out his reaction. He suddenly banged a hand against the steering wheel and let out a whoop!

"Runaway Express for sure."

The car jerked slightly when he did that. She grabbed the dashboard, turning back with a worried look.

"Sorry sorry."

"How long have you had your license?"

He glanced at her, and then brought a hand up to twirl an imaginary mustache. Nate said "License? We don't need no steenkin' LICENSE!"

She gave him a blank expression then a fake-shocked one and said "No license? Are you kidding me, we're riding with an unlicensed driver?"

"Unlicensed driver AND car thief, don't forget that.

Runaway too!"

They all laughed at how badass they were. The mood in the car brightened as Elsie exchanged smiles with Lou.

Elsie fell back into a light sleep.

CHAPTER NINE
GOOBER'S AUTO

Ten minutes later, Elsie woke in a panic, scared. She let out a deep groan then suddenly blurted out "I remembered it! Something was bothering me, earlier, and I just thought of it, Oh Nate, I should have thought of it sooner!"

He was puzzled, startled at her sudden dramatic turn, thinking NOW what?

"I saw a movie once and a guy, some crook guy stole a car. Well the cops were after him, after him driving the stolen car. And so the guy changed license plates! On the stolen car! That's us, right? Riding around in a stolen car that the cops are looking for, right?"

Nate's face went white. No shit, that's us!

He'd been vaguely worried that things were going too smoothly. Yeah, Dad will be pissed, he'll call the cops. Damn.

"Your Dad, he um, knows the license on the car. Probably right?"

"Yeah. Jeez, I'm such a dope for not thinking of it!"

This was bad, he felt. Real bad. He was getting scared

thinking what that meant. His shoulders slumped as his head dropped briefly. He grimaced and looked up.

"Thanks Elsie." And he meant it.

Because now that they know the problem, maybe they can DO something. The acknowledgement was appreciated but Elsie was alarmed. She turned her thoughts towards a license plate source. How the movie guy did it? She couldn't remember.

"Somewhere with a pretty full parking lot. Where we won't be noticed in the what, ten minutes? Fifteen it would take?"

He nodded, glad that she was already working on a solution.

"A mall? Um, factory? School? Where could we go?" Elsie was on to some possibilities.

Nate was thinking the same thing. "Maybe a parking ramp? At a hospital or some office building."

She wrinkled her forehead as she concentrated.

"There's cameras sometimes. Could we spot cameras?"

Nate's turn to frown.

Elsie looked out the side window. Nope, no malls or hospitals. Factories or office buildings either. Just snow-covered corn fields in West central Nebraska. Aware of the danger now, she felt like they were sitting ducks, a big ole target painted on the doors, a sign saying in bright bold letters 'THIS CAR IS STOLEN'.

Silence in the car for several miles. The snow had diminished to flurries, heavy in spots, then clear ahead. Nate kept his speed just under 60, focused on his headlights reaching out in front but also churning thru the implications and options of their suddenly perilous situation.

He said "Cameras, crap. They're everywhere."

Nate glanced at Elsie.

"Yeah." She sat up.

"But they aren't all watched, by like people, all the time I bet. At someplaces maybe, but not everywhere."

"Sure. Big places like malls or factories, they have security guards. Gas stations, the cameras probably just record."

"Hospitals - guards. Schools? Maybe grade schools. Regular streets, probably no cameras but..."

Nate thought about that. He'd sure hate to get surprised by some homeowner, some angry homeowner who was a firm believer in the Second Amendment. It'd take a lot of balls to do that, or maybe desperation, to do a dude's car in his street or driveway. He knew there had to be better options.

"OK so lots of cars or some anyway but no people, or no people after dark…. Or on weekends."

"Car lots!" she suddenly said.

"Yeah, yeah! But not the big new car dealers with the bright lights and stuff all night. Some little one, tucked away from the main streets. Goober's Auto or something."

"OK. So where exactly is Goobers? Ya gonna drive around all night, ya think that's safe Nate? Just circling around a strange town?"

Nate tensed up briefly, almost yielding to panic.

Lou piped up from the back.

"We're gonna get lucky. You guys will find the right one, and right away, I just know it."

Nate and Elsie burst into laughter. The black mood evident since the plates were brought up was lightened.

"Well thanks kid! It's reassuring to know we got your optimism going for us!"

Lou was prophetic. They got extremely lucky, taking the first exit off the freeway on the edge of Ogallala Nebraska.

It was an industrial area, some light commercial. A frontage road paralleled the Interstate, to their left, with a brightly lit truck stop anchoring the next exit. Nate was wrong, it wasn't Goobers, it was Midway Auto Sales. An unfenced business with 5 rows of cars, and as a bonus, an adjoining abandoned car wash. Bushes grew up at the shared edge of the two lots. Nate killed his lights and pulled into a spot behind a thick clump next to the car lot; out of sight but very accessible to Midway. He turned off the Cutlass.

"How are license plates attached?"

Nate wasn't sure. "Good question."

He slipped outside and checked out their traitorous tabs. Screws, bolts. He knew a little bit about mechanical stuff, he'd tinkered a little with his bicycle before. So tools, yeah, he figured a screwdriver would do it. He slid back into the Cutlass.

"We're gonna need some tools to get the plates changed."

Nate popped open the seat divider/arm rest, pawing thru its contents.

She joined the search and pushed the glove compartment button. The door flopped open.

Elsie screamed. Very loudly, right in Nate's ear.

She was frantically pointing at the cubbyhole. In a leather holster, with three loaded clips conveniently sitting alongside, lay a dull black pistol.

Nate's turn. "Wow!"

He knew Dad had guns, they'd shot this very same one out in the pasture. It was fun, one of the few things he and Angus enjoyed doing together. The boy was comfortable around the weapon but finding it in the car was completely unexpected.

"Wow? Really Nate, wow?" Elsie was aghast.

"It's OK Els, really! Dad and I shoot it at home, no big deal. Right now, we're still looking for tools."

He finished checking the glove box and closed it, ready to move on.

Once Elsie's shock wore off, a debate raged inside the Cutlass. Fumble in the dark replacing the plates and THEN get some sleep or grab a quick nap first? They had almost a half tank of gas, they could include that stop now too.

Nate wanted to search the car for tools in a lighted area and figured if they were recorded, it shouldn't be with the new and improved plates. He was willing to take the risk, now that they had located a safe place to get replacement ones. Elsie reluctantly agreed.

They motored over to the nearby truck stop and located a secluded spot to park. Nate got out and popped the trunk. It yielded a toolbox equipped with a basic set of hand tools including pliers and multiple screwdrivers. A winter survival kit added to their inventory. Tools - check. 3 fleece blankets, flares, candle – check. Lethal handgun and ammo – check.

He drove over to the pumps and gassed up; another sixteen dollars gone. When Nate and the girls went in to pay, he splurged for a foot-long BLT sub to share, surprising them as they returned from the bathroom. They waited for Nate to take his turn, talking briefly about their last truck stop visit.

Elsie joined Lou in the backseat when they returned to the Cutlass. It seemed wrong somehow for her to share the front seat with the boy. Wrong but exciting kind of too. Nate had no comment on the new arrangements, he just wanted to eat and sleep. They drove to a secluded parking area in back to eat their post-midnight meal, engine on, heater running. Nate distributed a bottle of water to each (thanks Dad!) to wash down the sandwich. They'd run out of things to say, other than goodnight. It was super warm inside, everyone was full. Nate turned the key, shut the car down. Each child got situated in their seats, under a blanket. They sat there undisturbed for the next three hours, getting some much-needed sleep.

Lou woke first, shivering in the cold. The car's warmth was long gone, her whole body was chilled. She shifted around under the thin blanket, tried to get her coat on with a minimum of movement, but the other two felt her struggles and stirred awake. Elsie, then Nate sat up, uncomfortable in the cold. A quick agreement; stop into the truck stop for one more restroom break before heading back to the car lot. It was 7AM. Still dark.

Nate started the car and drove up to the building where he sat, waiting for the girls to finish inside. They returned to the now warm Cutlass and he took his turn. Back much quicker than the girls, they idled out of the truck stop.

They pulled along side the third row of cars at the Midway lot and shut down, blending in. No security cameras evident, the few surrounding commercial buildings were unoccupied, there were no homes or apartment complexes within sight. The adjacent streets had no traffic. The three kids sat silent and dark in the Cutlass, alert and afraid, for 10 minutes.

As Nate prepared to slip outside, Lou realized the dome

light might give them away. She quickly slipped off her stocking cap and smothered the plastic cover; Nate exited so quickly he didn't even notice her assist.

The boy scuttled to the lineup in the back row. Dog Row his Dad called it. A quick survey indicated several cars with Nebraska plates. A beat-up Dodge Intrepid sat two cars over from the street. It looked like hard times but it sported plates with current tabs and what appeared to be new bolts holding them. Four minutes each, front and rear. Nate cradled the flat metal treasures under his coat as he made his way back to their Olds.

He briefly debated transferring his plates back on the Dodge but realized that there was zero benefit and would take extra time. No, the MN plates would have to disappear. 15 minutes later, after making the switch and dumping the incriminating outstate plates into a convenient storm drain, Nate re-entered the car, Lou covering the dome light again.

It was a huge relief. One big thing that could derail their getaway was taken care of. Once they'd realized the danger, they dealt with it. No need to itemize the remaining land mines, the odds against a successful outcome were probably overwhelming still. But they wouldn't go down in flames over out of state stolen plates. It was time to hit the road again.

Fueled up, rested up, with a fresh cloak of invisibility draped over their coach, the kids returned to the freeway, Lou now riding shotgun.

CHAPTER TEN
DO THE MATH

"Yeah. So, you said you were going to Vegas and stuff. Your girlfriend.." Lou got right to the point.

"NOT my girlfriend!" He quickly glanced into the back seat.

"Just a friend. From school. We hung out and had the same friends, four of us, and just kinda did stuff together."

"So she sent a ticket that your Dad ripped off and so you ripped him off, to get even. And you're gonna go out there, and, and THEN what?" Lou reached down to adjust the heater, just a little. Nate slapped her fingers lightly.

"Hey, what's that for!"

"Driver runs the temp, driver runs the tunes. He may let a lowly passenger mess with one or the other but I have NOT assigned any of that to you. Keep your grubby fingers off everything!"

They both laughed. Nate concentrated on driving for a bit, watching Lou out of the corner of his eye. She was looking at him, expectently. Waiting for her question to be answered.

"I don't know! Geez Louise, look around. I'm just wingin' it. Duh! I can't even believe I made it THIS far."

"We. WE made it this far Nate. Els said we're in. We're ALL in this together."

"But" she continued "I suppose we could be, um could be your HOSTAGES, yeah. You - armed and dangerous. Us just two damsels at your mercy, OH to be RESCUED!"

Elsie sat up murmuring "What're you bozos TALKING about?"

"Just goofing with your little sis."

Lou's turn to speak up. "We need to plan the next part of the trip. There's another interstate coming up, I-76. We either turn there or we don't so we gotta talk." Lou looked back at the map. "We need to talk about a couple things, I think."

Elsie leaned forward, her face between theirs.

"You're right Sis, let's talk. Me first. I've been thinking…"

Lou butted in. "Nate was just gonna tell us Els, weren't ya Nate, 'bout what we're doing, where we're going."

Elsie didn't like being interrupted, Lou was doing it more and more. But that WAS the best possible question.

"Yeah, Nate, Lou's right, let's talk about that. What IS the deal?"

They were both coming at him now, he was tag-teamed.

"I started out for Las Vegas, um two days ago, no yesterday, Friday, super early, and made it this far. WE made it this far. So we keep going I guess, I mean, either we keep going or we quit. Go back. And I don't wanna go back. So yeah. Gonna stop at, at, Denver, um, Cheyenne, well ya we get gotta figure out the BEST way to get there and, and, just, just KEEP GOING."

Nate and Elsie looked at each other, the boy looking determined, the girl with a frown.

"OK, say we figure out which way to go and by some miracle we don't die in a wreck or get pulled over, or a million other things, we get to Vegas. Somehow. THEN what Nate?"

Nate's turn to frown. "Well, it aint like we don't know anybody, I mean I guess ah we get there and I call her, and see what happens."

"Sam.", Elsie said, in a dismissive tone. .

"Yeah, Sam! Really, it's cool Els, you'll like her! Her Mom is cool, it'll all work out. I mean, I was invited and everything."

"We weren't."

That valid point shut him up for a moment.

"No no, it'll be OK, you'll see. We'll figure everything out. We ah, I dunno, should get rid of the car, stop driving it and stuff...

maybe call my Dad, I, I think it'll all be ok Els. Once we get there, we'll just kinda, go with the flow."

Elsie responded to his pleading eyes by crossing her arms.

Lou had another good question, looking at the open atlas.

"Um, you're looking at... 119... 270... ah something like, 900 miles to Las Vegas. From here. Do you have enough money Nate, money for gas to go that far, gas and everything? I mean, I'm sorry, it isn't like do WE have enough 'cause, WE got nothing. So it's how much do YOU have? How much for this trip?"

The boy was relieved to change the subject from Sam. "Go that far, hmm." He had no idea. He'd filled up one, two, yeah, twice, Des Moines and then Omaha. Got gas and the girls in Omaha. And a half tank in Ogallala, yeah..

"Uh, we got, 'bout seventy bucks, I think." He dug in his front pocket and pulled out a wad of bills. Elsie grabbed it and started counting.

Lou was looking at the map. "You started in Rochester, right?"

"Yeah."

"How much gas did ya have? Was it full?"

Nate thought back but couldn't remember.

"Dunno, why?"

"Where did ya get gas? I'm gonna figure out how far we can go. Oh and how much did you spend each time? On gas."

"Um, Des Moines, well not IN Des Moines, I think I waited til I was thru town, after getting on 80. Yeah. And ah, gas that time was, was 38 bucks!"

Lou did the math.

"OK, 38 bucks filled it?"

"Yeah, right to the top. Even slopped a little out, so yeah, full."

"And the next stop, next time ya filled up?"

"That's where I met the Klepto Carter sisters."

"Yeah yeah, very funny. Omaha. Filled it again?"

"Yeah full, and ah that was ah 35 bucks that time."

"Six and carry the one, 55 and.. "300 miles or so. A little less maybe. And with gas at two twenty, that's about 15, almost 16 gallons, into 300. 19 miles a gallon. 900 miles divided by ah 19, lets say 20 is 45 gallons to get to Vegas. So at two twenty, that's..."

"More than we got."

Elsie had finished counting.

"More than you guessed Nate but not enough more."

Lou said "A HUNDRED bucks we need. For gas, nothing else."

"We got eighty one, that's what you pulled outa your pocket Nate."

Crap crap crap. Nate slumped down. That was a bummer. He'd taken everything he had access to, he just figured he had PLENTY of money to make it, geez what a dummy. He thought back on what now, in hindsight, was dumb, unnecessary spending. The truckstop breakfast. The soda and chips, just that woulda been enough to make it up, have enough for gas. Maybe. What if gas is higher down the road, what if…

"Hand me the atlas Sis."

Lou handed it over the seat. Elsie was looking intently, flipping past the national map they'd been referencing, looking at the more detailed state maps.

"HA, well I was kinda right! Silverware for sure!"

Lou and Nate turned back to see Elsie, pointing at the map of Utah, with a big grin.

"Spanish FORK, not spoon or knife. Spanish FORK Utah!"

"Huh? What's THAT?" He was puzzled.

Lou got it, after a second. "You're right Els!"

"Nate, we may have an option, one that'll maybe fix the gas, er money, well the gas AND the money problem!"

"Yeah? What's that, you got a piggy bank stashed away? In Utah or something?"

"No, not a piggybank. But we maybe, MAYBE know somebody there, in Spanish Fork. Family! My aunt, our aunt. Mom's sister. We met her last year, she was, well she was really cool. And I remember being told, or hearing that she's in Spanish Fork. And that's before Vegas, kinda on the way, a detour sort of but maybe way before we run out of gas. IF we can make it that far and, I guess, IF we can find her. But it's something ya know. It's something!"

Nate nodded. It WAS something. Definitely something more realistic than getting all the way to Vegas, now that the dollars and distance were clearly understood. His plan was impossible, they needed an alternative.

So he said "Hey Brainiac, run the numbers. See if we can make to Spanish Fork on $81." Lou bent to the task after getting the atlas back from Els.

He concentrated on just how they could track down this

aunt of theirs. Library, phone book... well he COULD use his phone, do a search, but that would be the LAST resort.

"You DO know her name right, your aunt?"

"Yeah, kinda, its Traci with an 'eye' for sure but, last name could be Carter like ours but if she's married or WAS married.."

Great, Aunt Traci X, that'll really help finding her. Like they could check all the Tracy's and Tracie's to be sure. . .

Lou spoke up from the backseat. "Stay on 80, we meet 76 up ahead but we're gonna stay on 80, Interstate 80 West."

Sure enough, the two interstates met in a maze of lanes and signs. Nate was glad Lou was there to navigate for him. They kept to the right, following the signs for 80 and finally got back to a normal 4 lane. The sun was rising behind them, 140 miles to Cheyenne.

##

Blackie woke up in his Lazy-Boy, having dozed off watching 'Sports Center' 5 hours earlier. The chair was extremely comfortable, but it wasn't a worthy substitute for a regular mattress; his neck ached from an awkwardly positioned head.

He checked the time, Seven Thirty. Saturday morning. He could file the missing person's report in less than 2 hours. That gave him enough time to shower, shave and make coffee. He decided a fried egg sandwich would be the day's breakfast and 5 minutes later, he sat down at the dining room table to eat.

Nate's school picture was on the wall. Blackie wondered where he is RIGHT NOW, how he's doing. He worried that he might be scared or cold or hungry. Hurt. He didn't dare start imagining all the possible things that a teenage boy alone in a strange place could run into. Going down that line of thinking would only drive him nuts. He convinced himself that no news is good news, or at least meant no certified BAD news.

Finishing his meal, he brought the dishes back to the kitchen, rinsing them before neatly adding them to the dishwasher. Moving to his laptop, a quick once-through his favorite Ace of Spades blog assured him that no quakes had gone off overnight, SMOD still a no-show. End of the world postponed until some future TBD appearance.

Times up. It's been a day. He dialed the sheriff and got a different dispatcher than yesterday. 'Sheila – how-may-I-help-you' spoken rapidly across the line.

"Good morning Sheila, my name is Angus MacDonald. I called yesterday to report my car stolen. Today I want to file a missing person report on my 16-year-old son Nathan. Nathan, Nate MacDonald."

Sheila couldn't find a stolen vehicle report. After getting more info and referencing his rural address, Sheila finally did locate the 'vehicle moved without permission by a family member' report and put her caller on hold while she scanned thru it.

"You haven't heard from you son since....?"

"Thursday night. I spoke with him, barely, before we both went to bed. Or at least I went to bed, Nate apparently took some dead, white guy's advice to 'Go West young man, go West." His wit was lost on her.

It was Blackie's turn to ask a question.

"No reports of anyone spotting the car?"

"I'm afraid not sir. I'm looking at the case notes and the shift summaries. There's nothing in either."

She paused a beat

"We would have called you if any info came in overnight."

"Yes, thank you Sheila, I'm sure. It's just so damn hard waiting, not knowing what to do next. I'm really worried."

"Of course, Mr. MacDonald. Your frustration is perfectly

understandable. Kids run away all the time. They come home all the time too. "

"All of them Sheila?"

"No, not all. But the great majority do. Trust me, we see this sort of thing all the time. You'll get your boy back."

"Thanks, that's reassuring. A little. Anyway, I'd like to file a missing person report now. It's been 24 hours."

"Of course, Mr MacDonald."

After a half hour of re-telling yesterday's events, Blackie finally got a file number for one missing Nathan Archibald MacDonald. The data would flow swiftly from the local to the regional and finally to the national network of LEOs. Sheila didn't have the heart to tell Blackie about the hundreds of such reports her own dept received every week, and how they were pretty much utilized as a reference when an unknown or uncooperative citizen (or non-citizen) were encountered. The reports were NOT memorized at the start of each deputy's shift .

Naively, Blackie was under the impression that electronic alerts would spring into law enforcement inboxes around the country with Nate's info (and picture, they wanted him to bring in a recent picture). That would filter down to patrol units. It wouldn't be long now, every cop in America will be on the lookout for his son.

"Thanks again officer, you've been very helpful. I feel much better now that it's on record, Nate being missing. I'm confident he'll be back home very soon."

Sheila wasn't sure if he was being a sarcastic bastard or really meant it. They ended the call.

Blackie took down Nate's school picture and set it by the door. It would be good to get out of the house, to have a mission. The sheriff's office was really his only destination but that justified the trip to town. He got into his boots and jacket.

After locking the front door behind him, Blackie stood on his porch for a moment. A cigarette sure would hit the spot right now. He decided to start again, stop at the Kwik Trip and get a pack. He'd quit for years; well quit smoking daily anyway but occasionally would bum one. Yeah, I'll just quit again, after Nate is found. Blackie got into the pickup and headed to town.

Marlboro Special Blends at the North Broadway convenience store were NINE bucks a pack! That was about 2 bucks higher than the last time he bought one. Blatant gouging by the state, funding the billionaire's NFL palace on the lungs of

Minnesota smokers. Bunch-a thieves.

He grabbed some money out of the ATM and then stood outside, deciding if his plunge off the smoke-free wagon extended to lighting up in the truck. Probably, but not yet. The weather was improving, and he may as well get used to standing outside with the rest of the outcasts.

That first drag felt really shitty. He hacked a bit, took a couple of breaths and hit it again, even tho he was light-headed, almost dizzy. But he stuck with it, told himself hey, just like riding a bike.

Wonder where my son is. No call. Could he be lying in a ditch, car buried under snow?

These thoughts kept surfacing, unbidden, unwanted. Speculation wouldn't do any good, until there's some concrete information, I'm not gonna do the what-ifs. He consciously tamped those worries down, trying to find something else to think about. He walked back, finishing the cigarette at the smoker's pole. Geez, when was the last time I smoked? He got in the truck and belted up.

Two weeks ago? Yeah, James and I went to the range. The seatbelt rubbed on the cigarette pack in his shirt pocket, so he fished it out.

We sure shot the crap out of the Glocks that day. Good times. And that was the last time I smoked; I bummed one from him afterwards.

He reached over to open the cubbyhole of the truck, to stash the Marlboros. And it hits him, what was left in the cubby of the Cutlass, from that outing...

The handgun and ammo. OMG.

CHAPTER ELEVEN
BOLO FOR THE LEO

Angus walked up to the 2nd floor entrance of the Olmsted County Sheriff's office and stood at the security window. Behind the thick glass was a good looking female deputy, typing, while speaking into a headset. She acknowledged Blackie with an upraised finger and then quickly wrapped up both the conversation and the keystrokes. A speaker crackled.

"How may I help you?" Her nameplate read Patty.

"Hi Patty, I'm Angus MacDonald, I was told to bring in a recent picture of my son. Nate. Nathan MacDonald. He stole my car and took off for parts unknown yesterday."

He pulled out the school picture and placed it on the wide counter next to the security slot.

Patty started typing and glanced expectantly at her display.

She entered a few more taps and made a couple of mouse clicks.

A buzzing sound came from the door.

"Deputy Kasper is assigned to your case. Come in and take a seat in the room on your right, the deputy will be out to see you in a few minutes."

Blackie took a deep breath and entered, hoping his rising anxiety wasn't too evident. That goddam gun!

Signs indicated visitation rooms for meeting with those incarcerated in the jail complex below, cryptic entries with various department abbreviations, and meeting rooms 1 thru 4. He sat in the waiting room for several minutes, engulfed in institutional sounds and smells. A fit man with a shaved head arrived.

"I'm Deputy Kasper. You're Angus MacDonald?" He shook Blackie's hand and led him back into a room with a dozen or so cubicles. Half of the cubes were occupied by uniformed men and women.

"Have a seat Mr. MacDonald."

Blackie handed over Nate's photo and sat down in the proffered chair. The deputy sat at his workstation and briefly looked at the picture before sliding it into an envelope. He made a few keystrokes.

"We have a missing-person case open on your son now Mr. MacDonald."

"And the stolen-car report, that's still active, still being worked?"

"Well yes, the description of the vehicle has been sent out, we'll get a call when it turns up, but with the missing person status of Nathan, that ties in with the BOLO now."

Blackie wrinkled his forehead and shook his head slightly. "Bow-lowe?"

"Be On the Look Out sir. We're looking for both the car and the boy, where we find one, we'll probably find the other. I'll be sure Nathan's picture is out there and available to the units in the field."

The Deputy didn't reveal the low-to-non priority of it. Sure, if they spot the car, the runaway status will be linked but it will all be after the fact. No resources will be specifically deployed to find the kid, that's just the way it is.

"We haven't had any responses yet Mr. MacDonald. Do you have anything new to add, any contact or calls from the boy, any information from his friends, anything new you'd like to add?"

This was the moment to speak up about the gun. Blackie didn't hesitate, didn't waver from his firm decision made on the way over.

"No. Nothing. I was hoping you'd have some news for

me."

"When we do, you'll be contacted right away."

Blackie realized he was helpless, useless, power-less to influence the outcome. Law enforcement was too, to a large degree. They were poised to document the aftermath of whatever was going to happen, WAS happening right now somewhere South and West of here. Cops outline the body, they don't prevent the murder. He berated himself for the thought.

Blackie stood up and offered his hand. "I guess that's it then. Just stay by the phone, wait for your call?"

"Yes sir" They shook hands and Deputy Kasper led him back thru the maze, back to the door he started at.

"I'm sure he'll be found, found safe sir, they usually are."

He hoped his silence regarding the weapon was the right decision. It was something he'd have to live with, keeping quiet. But the gun WAS there, in the car. Was it better for the law to know about it, or not? God, he didn't know, he just PRAYED it works out, safely, quickly. Back in the truck, he lit a cigarette and rolled home with the window down.

His trip produced a BOLO for the LEO to go with the tracer on the cell-o. Blackie got up from his kitchen table and stretched his arms overhead. God, this is nerve racking. Stole my car, gun in the glovebox. On the road to Vegas, staying offline. I wonder when he last used the phone, or maybe when he last spoke with Sam... I shoulda got the info off the logs...

He brought up the Verizon site on his laptop. After some effort, he got into the account listing and with a little sleuthing, figured out Sam's number.

The records showed a call to Sam four days ago. Two days before Nate made his escape, D-day, departure day.

"What the hell, worth a try."

Blackie picked up his phone and punched in the number. Amazingly, after four rings, it was answered.

"Hello?"

"Hello Sam? This is Angus MacDonald; Nate's Dad. We met once or twice."

Silence.

He gave it the old 'and-a one and-a two'...

"Sam, Nate took off. I'm worried about him. He took my... well he's gone and I haven't heard from him. I think he, ah I'm PRETTY sure he's headed to Vegas. I wonder if you've maybe heard from him. Maybe?"

More silence.

"Please Sam. Anything? I'm worried.."

"YA THINK?? This really SUCKS, ya know? You STOLE Nate's ticket, kept it from him. It's ALL your fault!"

Blackie's turn to be silent.

"I DID talk to him, you're right, four days ago. He was mad. REALLY mad, about the ticket thing! But he said he had another way, that I should look for him and that he's coming. Didn't say how tho. You said he took.. what'd he take Mr MacDonald?"

"Nate stole my car Sam. He can't drive, doesn't have a license, doesn't know shit about driving. And it's a helluva long ways to Vegas. And crappy weather," he trailed off. "I'm so worried."

"You should be! It's your fault! And I'm worried, even more now too. God!"

"It's been almost a day and a half. I've filed a police report and have a trace on his phone. Nothing yet. Either he's stopped somewhere, hiding out or he's still on the road. On his way to you Sam."

The girl digested that. You can get a long way traveling for a day and a half, two days. Amazing really, to consider what Nate is up against; questionable driving skills, law enforcement, weather. Freaking amazing. And scary.

Angus made a snap decision.

"I'm coming Sam! I'm gonna see if there's any cash value from your, err, Nate's ticket. I'll pay ya back. Yeah, sitting around here is stupid, I'm gonna head out there."

"My Mom, you'll pay my Mom back."

"Whatever. He's probably closer to you in Vegas, being gone this long. I'll be there at the finish line to greet him. Yeah."

Or backtrack to pick up the pieces, a thought left unspoken.

"Um, sure... well OK I guess Mr MacDonald. My mom isn't here, but you two should really talk ya know?"

Blackie agreed to call back later. He's firm up the arrangements as much as possible with Colleen. They ended the call. Going to Vegas, yeah baby, me too. Sigh.

He pulled out the Bible the ticket was stashed in. Yup, yesterday morning. Blackie needed to get organized, find out his options, departure times and stuff. Thankfully he had Jo at Dream Vacations on speed dial. If anyone can pull this off, she can. Bless her heart, she answered on the second ring.

He raced thru the small talk and got to the point. And surprise, the unused ticket was worthless.

"My God Angus, you missed the goddam flight, you think any airline is gonna give you any kind of credit back for THAT?"

"And run that by me again about Nate, I can't hardly believe it, he did what?!" She was scanning the available flights as they talked.

He gave her the Cliff Notes version; like a lunatic I hid the ticket, he stole my car, cops, whoa. Jo worked her magic and got him on a flight that afternoon. She signed off with thanks, keep her informed, be safe. Ten minutes later, he was able to print off both boarding and shuttle passes in the name of Angus MacDonald. All legit and shit. Blackie started to pack.

CHAPTER TWELVE
MINNE-SNOWDA

The GoDirect shuttle was a little late. Angus had been dropped off at the downtown hotel pickup by his neighbor Larry, about 20 minutes earlier. Now, he slouched down in the lobby chair, trying to minimize contact with the annoying dude three seats to his right. He had an Irish complexion; freckles, pasty-white skin and red hair but combined with long greasy dreadlocks and a pronounced accent, he was severely out of place.

"Where I come from mon, the weather she ain gonna kill ya, ya know mon, just steppin' outside and shit."

"Yeah. It's Minnesota. In December 'n shit."

Hector, his name was Hector something-something, laughed loudly and threw a jab in Blackie's direction.

"Yeah man, Minnie-snowda."

Blackie had noticed the quirky character as soon as Hector walked thru the lobby doors. He watched as the man glanced around the room before smiling, nodding and walking directly over to Blackie's sectional seating. He made an elaborate display of situating his large briefcase and backpack on a chair next to Blackie's backpack and small duffle.

Hector wore sweat pants and newish looking tennis shoes. He topped it off with a tee shirt and an unlined windbreaker. Unzipped of course. Absent hat and gloves.

They were both waiting for the same shuttle, about 5 minutes late now. This lobby was the last pickup before hitting HWY 52 for the hour-long trip to MSP International.

They exchanged typical bits of insignificant travel info, Hector just passing thru to go 'home overseas', Angus to 'meet his son'.

A white van pulled up. Blackie stood and took several steps forward to confirm it was for them. He took a moment to bend and stretch, prepping for the upcoming confinement. Hector clapped him on the shoulder as he passed by, heading for the door.

"C'mon mon, doan wanna miss teh bus!" followed by a cackle.

No indeed, let's get this show on the road. Blackie gathered up his belongings and went outside.

The driver had the rear doors open, waiting for these last two passengers. He had just stuffed Hector' briefcase in an upper compartment when Blackie approached.

"Stow your bag sir?" while reaching for it. Blackie handed it over and glanced into the van. Not bad. Decent looking captains seats, most of them populated. His newest acquaintance was in the back row, grinning and patting the seat next to him. Blackie raised a hand in acknowledgement and figured why not, what could it hurt? He stepped over to the side door and settled in the seat across from Hector. His backpack easily fit underneath. The driver, Dan according to his nametag, buttoned up the vehicle and climbed behind the wheel. Light snow began falling as they pulled away.

"Thank you for choosing GoDirect today. My name is Dan. With these road conditions, we'll be at the main terminal in 65 minutes. 1:40. The wifi password is GODiRECT12. If you have any questions, feel free to speak up and thanks again for choosing GoDirect folks."

The interior was comfortably warm. Blackie wished he'd taken a couple of pepto-bismol tabs before leaving. He'd skipped breakfast, didn't want to dirty the kitchen. Had a warmed-over cup of yesterday's coffee before leaving and it appeared that may have been a mistake; his stomach was rumbling. Oh well, they'll have bathrooms and food at the airport. No problem. 65 minutes.

"Look at da crazy weather mon, dam it be snowin again!" Hector was leaning across Blackie's lap, rapping on the window glass for emphasis. Tap Tap Tap.

"Minne-snowda Hector. We have a saying for that. Uff da."

Hector leaned back and laughed and laughed. "Yeah mon, Uff da mon, y 'all be crazee crazee!"

Blackie closed his eyes. He wondered what Nate was doing right then, and where he was, if he was alright. A hand on the inside vest pocket of his jacket confirmed he had his phone. No calls. No news. He hoped the old saying is true, regarding Nate at least. No news is good news. He sighed, hoping to catch a catnap.

Hector pulled out a smart phone and focused on the tiny screen. All the passengers settled into their own cocoons as the van made its way across town. It merged onto the four lane and headed northwest, towards the airport and destinations beyond.

Dan the driver's estimate was off by 2 minutes. They pulled up to the terminal at 1:38, which gave Blackie over an hour before his flight would board. Plenty of time. He started taking inventory of the items he'd brought; phone still in the inside pocket, his wallet in a front pocket of his jeans. Nothing else really mattered. He glanced around at his fellow riders; they were fiddling with their stuff, setting carry-ons on their laps, looking out the windows.

Several people were gathered outside the van's passenger doors, which remained closed. Dan was already up and out his side, speaking with someone at the rear of the van. A well- built man was leaning back against the side doors, arms crossed, his clean-shaven head at eye level of the seated passengers. He was watching some guy just finishing up a conversation with their driver, behind the van. A murmur buzzed thru the passengers. Blackie was wondering what the delay was and where the closest bathroom might be. Hector was suddenly sweating, craning his head to see outside.

Dan now stood about 10 feet behind the van, in front of a black SUV that was blocking the inside lane at the terminal. People swarmed in and out of the building, cars, taxis and buses wheeled around the bottleneck the GoDirect shuttle created. A few horns blared.

A 30-ish, slightly built man wearing jeans, a hooded sweatshirt and a dark ball cap opened the side doors, standing there, looking at each passenger in turn. He reached inside his shirt and pulled out a long necklace chain, a shiny badge centered at the bottom.

"My Name is Detective Peterson. I work for the state of Minnesota. We'll be moving you and your belongings to an inside checkpoint and then you'll be on your way. One at a time please folks"

He pointed to the 65-year-old man closest to the door and waved for him to step outside. Once the senior citizen had exited, a uniformed officer walked him thru the terminal doors. The detective then motioned for the next passenger to get out.

"What's dis bullshit?" Hector had turned towards Blackie, still whispering, "Oh no, fuck that checkpoint mon!" The happy/dopey persona was gone.

Alarmed, Blackie turned to look at his seatmate. The man was agitated, with rapid breathing, jerky nervous mannerisms and flopsweat beading up on his forehead. He almost hummed with tension.

DING DING DING! – bells started exploding in Blackie's brain. What in the everlasting fuck is going on!!?

His stomach did a lurch as he started processing his situation; cops + agitated suspect = possible collateral damage.

Everyone else had gotten off, their stowed luggage carried away by one of a multitude of security people that suddenly milled thickly around outside. The Detective pointed at Blackie next, apparently wanting Hector to be the last one off.

Blackie, his mind racing, took a deep breath and slowly reached down between his legs to snag his backpack. He shouldered the bag and looked at Hector before he squeezed by; the man's fists were balled up tightly, one knee bouncing rapidly up and down. He didn't acknowledge Blackie, his eyes were focused outside, across the lanes of traffic.

A plainclothes officer relieved Angus of the leather bag as soon as he set foot outside. His duffle was on the ground next to them. Pointing to it, he said "Is this yours?"

Blackie nodded. He was led to the nearby door and then stopped and patted down, facing the building. He'd never been frisked before, decided he didn't like it, didn't like what it meant at all. His wallet was handed to another cop who examined Blackie's driver's license intently.

"I'm sorry officer. My guts are churning. Bad coffee, this crazy shit this morning, I mean, frisked, my God. And heartburn like you wouldn't believe, I gotta get to a sink or a toilet, and…"

Shouts, the sound of people running.

"Stop! STOP GODDAMMIT!!"

Behind them at curbside, Hector had shoved a cop to the ground and was making a mad dash for the parking ramp across from the terminal. Horns blared and tires squealed as eight lanes of traffic reacted. Officers quickly took up pursuit, radios crackling and weapons out, trying to close the twenty yard gap.

The fleeing man hopped the low outer wall of the open rental/parking ramp structure and headed into the interior darkness. Three cops followed 6 seconds behind, their cries of STOP STOP! now echoing off the concrete walls.

Blackie had turned and watched in disbelief as the crazy events played out. Suddenly he hears "Freeze God Dammit, DON'T YOU MOVE" which was instantly followed by a smashing blow from behind. He went down to the ground, hard.

A heavy force ground his face into the sidewalk. Blackie couldn't help it, the pressure on his stomach was too great. He threw up a watery spew that dribbled down his cheek and pooled on the concrete. He was spitting and trying to catch his breath after the blow to his ribs,

A pissed off cop leaned in close. "Well isn't this just great.

Your jerkoff buddy makes us fucking chase him... What's his reason to bounce like that? What's this all about Mr. MacDonald? What's the goddamn deal with you two?"

Blackie assumed it was a rhetorical question. He wasn't going to answer, because answering would involve movement and the last thing he was told was Don't Move.

The weight on his back shifted. He was maneuvered into a sitting position, arms gathered behind him, and then finally cuffed, all with his full cooperation. Strong arms assisted him to his feet. He had just turned to face the detective who stood there giving his prisoner the stink eye when shots suddenly rang out.

Three of them, from different sounding weapons. Blackie flinched, the officer grimaced and took off running across the street, barking orders into a lapel mic.

Radios crackled with sharp voices from the half dozen law enforcement squads in the vicinity. Vehicles with flashing lights were racing around on multiple levels in the ramp, the strobe effect providing a surreal element to the scene. The horns and sirens deafened him as he watched the action unfold. His back throbbed, he could tell his nose and forehead were scraped, blood and puke dripped from his swollen lower lip. He slipped back down to the sidewalk and leaned against the wall with eyes closed.

After a moment of reflection, and feeling sorry for himself, he realized things could be worse. His morning was still going much better than Hector's.

Uff da mon.

A cop grabbed his collar and pulled Blackie to his feet. He was hustled inside, away from the chaos raging in the parking ramp. A doorway off the main terminal led to a behind the scenes hallway which led to an unmarked holding room They'd brought him here and shut the door about 20 minutes earlier.

He was still cuffed, but in front now, a big improvement. Blackie sat on a chair that was bolted to the floor at a table that was bolted to the floor. He'd been frisked again, thoroughly, prompting him to ask about maybe a bathroom visit? No response, other than a laugh. Should have saved his breath,

He laid his head down on his handcuffed arms. This is a fine mess Laddie; missed the flight, got arrested, even threw up on yerself. How the hell can I go get Nate if I'm sitting in jail?? And WTF, I didn't do nothing to get arrested. That goddam Hector, damn him! I shoulda known, shoulda kept my distance. What was

I thinking, getting all chummy, sitting with him, in the lobby AND on the shuttle?

Freakin' Hector, I wonder what's up with the gunshots. Man I did NOT see that coming. He was squirrely when we were sitting there, at the end, 'fuck the checkpoint' or something. Man. Oh shit, I sure hope he didn't shoot a COP, shit, they'd suck ME into that sure as hell... Oh man I'm SO screwed..

The door flew open. A very agitated Detective Peterson came over to the table and SLAMMED his hand down.

"I'm gonna make your life hell MacDonald, make you wish you'd never been born, unless you start telling the truth, right here, right now!" He glared at Blackie across the gap.

THINK dumbass, think before you open your mouth, this guy wants your nuts for a trophy... do I tell the truth or... wait a minute. I don't have to make up any story, I don't have to explain nothing, the truth is what it is. Yeah, I don't need to make up some explanation, get tripped up on some stupid lie. If I start at the beginning, just start there... just tell the goddam truth!

"You know my name, where I live Detective. I'm sure I've been thoroughly checked out. You probably know my credit score; I don't." The cop continued the evil-eye at Blackie. "I left my home in Rochester this morning, got a ride into town from a neighbor. Got on the shuttle to come up here with the intention of boarding a plane. To go get my son. My runaway son, did I mention that detective?"

Peterson knew all that. MacDonald was a rube, a civilian. The lobby tape clearly showed Hector stuffing a small bundle into MacDonald's backpack, sneaking it in while Angus had his back turned. But he did have MacDonald for possession, the Ecstasy was found in his baggage. He could bust him, just to fuck with him. He could.

"Tell me about your traveling companion, the Marathon Man. You've met him before right, you two knew each other."

Blackie sighed.

"You know the answer to that too. First time I saw him was in the hotel lobby. C'mon, I know you or your people have the tapes. Did we strike you as old friends?"

"Are you gonna tell me, in your own words, how it is you two came to be sitting together on the shuttle all buddy-buddy, and before that, in the lobby. C'mon yourself, humor me. Start from the beginning."

So Blackie did start from the beginning, all the way back to hiding the ticket. Stole my car, went to Vegas, whoa... and then, to the point, how he'd been in the lobby when Hector came in. How it was creepy that the guy came over, crowded into HIS space, acted a little too..friendly or something. And the seating situation on the shuttle, last stop, last ones to get on, all quite innocent officer.

"That's all I know about Hector, swear to God. I'm sure you know much more detective. Is he some master criminal, wanted by Interpol, a terrorist you guys have been tracking forever, what is it, who is he?"

"He's a chump, a lowlife wannabe gangbanger. Grew up in Jamaica, Daddy was an ambassador. And yes, wanted for smuggling drugs thru diplomatic pouches. A whiteboy rasta-man. But now, a dead one."

Blackie shuddered and looked away. Dead? Wow.

"Yeah, we saw the tapes. He was fucking with you, he scoped you out in the hotel, stuffed some pills into your backpack. Not sure why, if you DID get thru the screening, was he gonna meet back up to get 'em back? Not likely, not for 50 hits of 'X'."

Blackie was gobsmacked. Damn! Wouldn't that be the surprise of his day, hell, his LIFE, to have some TSA goon pull drugs outa my backpack. That fucker!

"I think he maybe forgot he had 'em til he got to the hotel. Instead of dumping them, he decided to have some fun, mess with the doofus guy, probably hang back and watch."

Ouch. Doofus, that's harsh.

"But why'd he run Detective, why take off?"

"He has an outstanding warrant, he's a person of interest in a couple of things, it was just a matter of time. We made him back in Rochester, thought we might reel in some bigger fish. Then, he's on his way to the airport and we were curious where he was headed."

A pause,

"Are you a bigger fish Mr MacDonald?"

Blackie laughed and shook his head. He looked at the officer and laughed again.

"No, I am not. Nope, nada no sir. I'm just a big doofus looking for his kid. A guy who sat by the wrong dude. A now dead dude."

He continued "Wrong place at the wrong time. That's me, what a loser. Can't even catch a plane without fucking it up. My flight is gone baby, and instead of being on it, on my way to my son, I'm sitting in handcuffs, arrested because of drugs in my carry on." He finished. "I'm sure big fish have their shit together better than that, officer. Damn sure."

Detective Peterson paused briefly, then produced a key for the cuffs. He bent down to release Blackie, knowing the man spoke the truth.

"There's plenty of other planes to catch you know. You never were arrested, just detained. Nothing on your record, just an hour or so out of your life. So nothing's changed, really, for you. Not a great day maybe but not as bad as Hector's."

Blackie felt a flood of relief. He's right! He wasn't stopped, only delayed. Nate is still out there, still on the run. I can pick up the pieces here, gather myself, get my butt out to Vegas yet. The door opened. His duffle and backpack were sitting on the floor in the hallway.

He stepped toward the door and was blocked by the outstretched hand of Detective Peterson. Blackie stopped to shake it.

"No hard feelings I hope. Godspeed and good luck Mr. MacDonald." He stuffed a business card in Blackie's shirt pocket.

Thanks, Blackie thought, I need both.

CHAPTER THIRTEEN
BRIGHT LIGHTS, DASH LIGHTS

Something had changed, he noticed the difference out of the corner of his eye. Nate zeroed in on the dash board- OH NO, the check engine light came on! CRAP! He was sure, no he was POSITIVE it wasn't on before. It must have just happened. The boy dragged his eyes upwards to scan the roadway ahead, then rolled thru his mirrors. He took another glance at the dash, hoping against hope that the light would now magically be dark. No such luck.

Elsie noticed Nate's mood change. "What's wrong?"

He glanced over, his distress obvious.

"Oh man, this is bad!" and pointed to the lights.

"What's it say, CHECK ENGINE... oh geez Nate, now what?"

His panic level ratcheted up a notch. Car trouble wasn't on the radar before but now it was the ONLY thing he could think of; this is really terrible! His heightened senses picked up a faint rhythmic ticking sound, just at the edge of hearing. Was his mind playing tricks or was that an audible confirmation of the light's message? Over the course of five minutes he convinced himself it was growing slightly louder.

Another 25 miles with the noise and the red light on. They were closing in on Cheyenne, now forty to go. Suddenly another ominous light came on. Oil! His attention was completely distracted to the escalating bad news coming from his dashboard.

Those last miles were nerve racking. The engine noise continued but seemed unchanged, or at least Nate didn't think it was getting any louder. Maybe because the one thing he wanted most in the whole world, right now at least, was for that sound to not get any louder. No that wasn't true, he really really wanted it to quit and for both warning lights to go out. But if he couldn't have that, he'd take it not getting worse.

Nate watched the temp gauge as closely as he watched the road ahead. He thought they could maybe get to the truck stop OK, check the oil, actually ADD oil, and maybe it'd be OK. To keep going. Adding oil was probably something they could handle themselves, even tho there goes more money they can't afford.

But if she (when did he start thinking of the car as female?) if she overheats, they were probably screwed. End of the line. And that gauge was cooperating so far, sitting right in the middle, right where it'd been the whole trip.

He spotted the exit ramp up ahead. The truck stop was a

bright oasis to the left, on the other side of the freeway. It was looking good, his spirits rose.

"I think we're gonna make it ladies!"

Squeals from the girls. "Never a doubt!" from Elsie, an "Amen!" from Lou. Nate hit the blinker and navigated off the freeway, stopping at the top to give a semi the right of way. They got across the bridge and entered the truck stop.

He decided to gas up first, check the dipstick while doing that. There were 5 rows of pumps; he chose the one furthest from the building. Elsie was dispatched to the cashier with $40 of their dwindling reserves, Lou tagged along. Nate had the hose in the tank, waiting for the pump to be authorized, as a small motor home pulled in behind him.

Gas started flowing. Nate opened the driver's door and peered under the dash, looking for something to unlatch the hood.

There were two tabs there, each with a cryptic graphic. It was kinda too dark to read 'em; he decided to yank one. Jackpot!

He stepped back out. An older woman was fueling the RV. Nate nodded to her and walked around to the front. The hood had popped up about an inch. He stuck his fingers in the opening and tugged. Nothing. What the heck? He bent down and examined the gap, and then looked over the grill closely. Another tug on the hood confirmed that yup, something was still holding it. He gave it another try, frustrated.

"You gotta open another one, the safety latch."

The woman with the motor home had walked up alongside the Cutlass. "It's a lever or a tab, inside, under the hood usually."

Nate fumbled around, searching, probing his fingers along the lip of the hood. There! The released hood popped up a foot, he raised it the rest of the way. But it wouldn't stay. He moved it up and down a couple time, hoping it would catch, but it didn't.

"There's a rod, folded up inside. That's what holds it up. There's a hole in the hood, stick the rod in it."

Nate felt like a dumb little kid. He peered inside and quickly saw it, then fitted it into one of several openings in the underside of the hood.

"Gee thanks. I haven't had to open 'til now, ha. Hi, I'm Nate, er, Nathan." The boy stuck out his hand.

"Pleased to meet 'cha Nathan. I'm Mary. You probably woulda figured it out." A charitable assumption.

She stuck out her hand, the boy smiled and shook it. Nate

turned to look at the engine, wondering about the oil situation. He didn't know anything about cars and was wishing he did. Mary sniffled, then politely coughed into the hand Nate just shook.

The pump dinged off. He brushed off his hands, excused himself, and walked back to the hose. $34.19, just under 15 and a half gallons. He squeezed the nozzle and topped it off at $35. The girls would bring a five back. Good.

Mary was leaning under the hood when he returned to the front.

"What's the problem Nate?"

"Um, the engine light, the red check engine light came on. Then the oil light. That was like, 15 miles back. I didn't know if we'd make it. And then, the engine started making a noise and I REALLY didn't think we'd make it."

"We? Who are you traveling with son, your folks?"

Think fast, Nate. They'll be out here in a second.

"Um, sisters, Elsie and Lou. The girls are riding with me."

He avoided looking Mary in the eye. She turned back to the engine. "The first thing is to check the dipstick. It's this long thing here." Mary reached in and pulled it out. Bare. Foamy. She had Nate grab a paper towel off the pump island, which she used on the dipstick. She then plunged it back into the motor and waited. She asked

"That's nice that you're traveling with your sisters, how old are they?"

Nate gulped.

"They're ah, let's see, Elsie is 16 and Lou is, about 11, yeah 11 I guess."

"So they're your younger sisters. That would make you, what, 17?"

Elsie came up just then; perfect timing!

"Elsie, boy am glad to see you. This nice lady is Mary, she's helping me figure out the oil thing. I ah, I wouldn't even have the hood open if she hadn't saved the day. She, um, she asked, ah, I told her that we were all traveling together, and a, say, where is Lou?"

"She's right behind me, see?" Sure enough, Lou showed up, a five-dollar bill clenched in her hand.

Elsie greeted the older woman, as did Lou, still holding the five.

"Well isn't this nice, a brother and his sisters traveling together. Where ya going kids?"

Nate spoke up quickly as the girls exchanged puzzled looks. "We're going out West. For, for Christmas! Really looking forward to it. Say, what about that dipstick Mary?"

She eyeballed all three kids before turning her attention back under the hood. The dipstick had just a hint of oil at the very bottom tip. She showed Nate, then the girls.

"You ran it out of oil. That's hard on 'em. It'll take at least a couple of quarts to get it filled up again."

"Will it be ok, I mean once we get oil back in, we can keep going right?" Nate was needing some reassurance.

"Hard to say. For sure you won't get another 10 miles unless you DO put oil in. So you kids are all alone? How much farther, where ya headed?"

Questions, questions, Nate didn't know what to say, he was tired and scared and didn't want to blurt out something, something STUPID, that would get them turned in.

Lou to the rescue.

"We're going to Utah Mary, to our Aunt's house in Spanish Fork. It's about, oh, another 500 miles we think."

Elsie and Nate exchanged relieved looks. Lou sounded convincing.

Mary's pump dinged, her RV was gassed, at a total considerably higher that the car's.

"That's me. Well kids, that's still a long ways to go. And especially now with you having car trouble. Nate, go get a couple quarts of oil."

She reached in and twisted off the oil cap on the engine. "Pour both bottles in here, be careful not to be sloppy with it. Put the oil cap back on and we'll let it work its way thru the engine, then check the dipstick again. First things first tho. They don't want us plugging up the pump islands, let's move both rigs out back."

He put the cap back on and slammed down the hood.

"You drive over and get the oil. We'll be in the back, come over and park next to us. Open this back up like I showed ya, add that oil. We'll have some supper made, OK?" She gave his arm a squeeze, then turned to the girls

"Ladies, we'll move to the back row, then your brother will join us. Hop in, door's around there, let me show you the inside."

As the three females walked away together, Mary had one last instruction.

"5W 20 boy, the oil, 5 doub-you twenty!"

Mary coughed again, then put her arm around Lou. She led the girls to the back, unhooked the hose and then walked around to enter the motor home thru the side door. Nate watched them. Gee, should I be worried, suppose she's stranger danger or something? She could take off. She could.. Nate knew, in his heart, that Mary posed no threat. Besides, I bet those two girls could put up a fight. Maybe I should be worried about Mary.

He laughed and drove up to the truck stop, wondering how much a couple quarts of oil could possibly cost; a buck a piece, maybe the same as a gallon of gas, couple bucks? Whatever, it'd put a further dent in their funds. He started doing the math, wondering how much was left as he entered the building.

CHAPTER FOURTEEN
SOME BACHELOR PARTY

"Dream Vacations, this is Jo." Her upbeat tone raised Blackie's spirits immensely.

"Hey Jo, this is Blackie again. Ha ha, hey I ah, I missed that flight! It's a crazy story let me tell ya, but anyway, can you get my butt on another plane? Like, now, today?"

"BLACKIE, missed your flight, what the hell? I like crazy stories, spit it out!" She was already keying up the Interwebz.

"Um, well there's drugs, and handcuffs.. and a dead guy"

Maybe too much information.

"Wow, that was some bachelor party huh? Hey Southwest, flight 419. Leaves at 5:10, Gate C22. DEAD GUY, OMG, yer such a kidder, ah gets into Vegas at 5:30. Say the word, it's yours"

"Word"

"Done deal. So no news from Nate yet?"

"Nope. Plans the same, head him off. I should get alerted if his phone gets used, or if the cops spot him, or..."

"Don't worry, he'll be fine. You're doing the right thing. DRUGS Huh? You ARE full of surprises. Wow. Well stay away from that crap. Be safe, Angus, find Nate, bring him home. Let me know if ya hear ANYTHING, alright? Promise?"

Angus got a few more details about the flight, assured Jo he'd keep her updated, and then gathered his luggage. He'd been offered coffee and a doughnut by the cops which he declined and was then released inside the TSA checkpoints, on the edge of a concourse. Across a stream of hurrying people and noisy activity, a pizza franchise tormented his nose.

Gate C22, 5:10, that gave him 55 minutes to get on a flight. Attempt number two for those keeping score at home.

He realized he maybe shoulda had the doughnut. After a bathroom stop, he'd grab a sandwich on the way to his gate.

A men's room fifty feet down the concourse provided a sink and mirror for checking his appearance. The crusted blood and puke were cleaned off easily enough but the actual cuts and bruises remained. He had a fleeting thought that this is how a survivor of a car accident might look before examining his clothing. The nylon parka shell had his drool, easily removed. His pants were scuffed a bit at the knees which Angus brushed off as best he could. Another once over and he deemed himself presentable. He gathered his carry-ons and exited.

'Chic-Fil-A' provided the sandwich, in fact two, along with a chocolate shake. He ate at a table, watching the parade of people on the concourse. What a variety, what an infinite number of reasons that brought them to this spot, right now. It was relaxing, having 10 minutes to sit down, to leisurely savor a tasty lunch, to be a free man again.

Wow.

He shook his head, recalling the past few hours. Hector dead. Uff da. He wondered what Nate was doing right then, where he was at. Blackie pulled the phone out to check, nothing. OK kiddo, comin' to git ya, ready or not.

He gathered up his stuff, dumping the meal trash in a receptacle and headed back out on the concourse. Gate 22 was about 100 yards ahead.

Blackie walked up to the counter to get his boarding pass. It appeared the plane would start loading in 15 minutes, plenty of time.

He pulled his billfold out and presented his MN driver's license to the agent. "Angus MacDonald."

The agent, Margie according to her nameplate, typed a little and then took a second look at the license. She tapped a couple more keys and then looked at Blackie, smiling.

"Just one moment Mr. MacDonald."

She picked up a phone and punched in a number, waiting with the handset to her ear.

Blackie is bewildered. Now what? Good ol Marge turned away and spoke briefly into the phone before hanging up.

"If you can step over here Mr. MacDonald?" pointing to the other end of the counter.

"Is there some kind of problem Margie? I'm here for a boarding pass to flight 419. The next one departing from this gate amiright?" He made a show of peering at the gate posting.

"Yup, 419, sez so right there."

"Mr. MacDonald?"

A pair of security goons were suddenly flanking Blackie, sandwiching him between them. One leaned over

"Sir, please move with us over here. Please."

They two men guided Blackie along and past the counter. Several people behind Blackie in line gawked at the spectacle.

Not again. It can't be. I, I...

"Mister MacDonald, your name was flagged in the database, that's why we were contacted. You sir, are not supposed to get on a plane."

"You gotta be fucking kidding me!" His outburst caused the two burly men to move into position to easily neutralize whatever might come next. Realizing how he sounded, Angus moderated his tone and attitude. "Listen, let me ask, please check, was that recent, like today, couple hours ago? I can explain, or even better…"

He fished the detective's card out of his pocket and handed it over. "Call this number, just call it. Please?"

Each officer got on his phone, one checking on the timestamp of Blackie's arrival on the no-fly list. The other one punched in the number off the card and began a conversation.

Blackie stood there, knowing he was caught up in a government FUBAR, angry but resigned to his helpless fate yet again. The security team shut down their phones at about the same time.

One said "He hit the list two hours ago."

The other one said "Detective Peterson apologizes for the oversight, you are no longer on the list. Carry on sir."

The cop gave a thumbs up to the counter agent after giving Blackie back the card. Marge nodded.

He returned to the line and got behind several other passengers, who kept their distance and appeared uncomfortable. Finally, he was back where he started, facing the gate agent again.

"Will you be needing my license again Marge?"

"Thanks Mr. MacDonald but I already have all your information right here."

A printer spit out the coveted boarding pass. She handed it to him with a faint smile. He turned to find an open seat in the waiting area.

Before Blackie could pick out a chair to plop into, he heard the announcement that first class is now boarding. He checked his ticket; First Class! He murmured 'Love you Jo' as he jumped up and strolled to the jet-way. His fellow passengers took note of their flight's first class, looking for someone famous.

Screw you plebes he thought as he joined the short line of fellow elites. Just what he needed, something to go right for a change. He was led to a wide luxurious seat up front, offered a pillow and had his drink order taken – Bloody Mary if you please.

He sipped the cocktail as the low-class shuffled back to their seats in the cattle section. One thought ran thru his mind.

What next Lord, what next..

CHAPTER FIFTEEN
LONG DAY

Four BUCKS a quart! What a rip-off. Nate was steamed at having to pay that much. The automotive section had a bewildering array of offerings. He found the fluids and narrowed his gaze to a seemingly endless variety of motor oils. Different brands, different.. numbers or something. 5 something. He looked closer, they all had W numbers, what was it. Yeah, 5W 20, that's what she meant.

There were a bunch of different kinds; synthetic, high mileage, different prices. He zeroed in on the 5W 20's and picked not the most expensive but not the cheapest. Still at $3.95 each it seemed like a LOT. But Mary was right, had to have it to keep going. Just like he had to have some sleep for him to keep going. Five hundred more miles.

He wistfully looked at snacks at the checkout when paying for the oil then remembered supper was promised in the motorhome. Nate went back out and pulled his hood tighter as he approached the Cutlass. He threw his purchases across the seat as he got behind the wheel and closed the driver's door.

A hesitation as he sat in the dark and silent interior. He

fished out the key and inserted it. Maybe the noise would be gone, the dash lights dark this time. He cranked the ignition and had a new fear as the starter turned over, and over. Maybe she won't even start!

She did. Start that is. Finally. But the awful clattering noise was still there, the alarming lights on the dash were still lit. But she did start.

He turned the lights on and eased away from the brightly lit building. The RV was easy to find in the back row. It sat in an opening between two wind-blocking semi's, with a space waiting for the Cutlass opposite the side door.

Nate popped the hood release and got out. He peeked in the window of Mary's motor home. She and the girls were seated around a dinette table, eating crackers and cheese, open Cokes in front of all three. It looked warm and homey. Nate tapped on the window and waved, holding up the oil. They all waved back, looking like they were getting along just dandy. Mary pointed to herself, asking if he needed her to come out. He shook his head no.

The boy hurried to the front of the car. The sooner this was done, the sooner he could get inside. The hood was blocking much of the available light once he got it open. He fumbled a bit twisting off the oil filler cap, then felt for the opening, ah there. He got the first quart opened but the goofy neck on the bottle confused him; he was a little sloppy getting it poked in there. He watched and listened as the container glugged out its contents. When he was sure it was empty, he repeated the process with the second one.

He threw the empties into the plastic bag he bought them in, and placed it on the floor of the car. It took several attempts to get the oil cap back on the engine. He imagined the oil coursing thru the block, finally pooling in the bottom. He wondered how long to wait.

"You did good kid, close it up and c'mon inside with us."

Mary was right there, had checked his work, and nodded approvingly. He gave the engine compartment a once over, then slammed the hood. The cold and tired boy walked with her to the RV.

Elsie and Lou scooted close to make a spot for Nate on the end. He stood there as Mary removed her coat and boots, then stood next to Elsie.

"Take your coat off, your shoes too, put 'em by the door"

Nate did as he was told, then slid in next to Lou.

"Coke, water? What'll you have?"

Nate was suddenly thirsty, hungry too.

"Coke please."

The woman retrieved a cold can from her small fridge and placed it in front of him. Mary took a seat next to the oldest girl. A silence fell over the table.

"I've had a nice visit with your sisters Nate. It sounds like you've had a long day."

She stared at him expectantly. Nate looked at the girls, wondering what exactly they had told her. Lou spoke up.

"Mary says this is a good place to park for the night Nate, in the back here, by the big trucks. She ah, she was wondering what we we're gonna do? Tonight, I mean. We told her you'd been driving a lot, stressed about the engine trouble, that we're all kinda tired."

Lou turned to look at Mary, who gave her a nod.

"She said, if we wanted to, if it's OK with you and all, we could have supper together now. Then she said we could spend the night! In here, all of us, in real beds! Instead of, you know, sleeping in the car again."

Nate looked around. He'd never been in a motor home before. There was a pretty good size loft kind of deal above the front seats, and what looked like a real bedroom in the back. So Mary back there, the girls up top... he was tired and wondering where that left him. Not that it mattered, anything would be better than another cold night in the car. And he did have to sleep, he was really dragging. But he somehow felt obligated to decline her offer. At least once.

"That's real, real nice Mary but we don't want to be any kind of bother or anything."

"Yes, it IS really SUPER nice Nate. And we already told Mary that she didn't have to, we were fine and everything, but.." Her voice trailed off.

Elsie finished Lou's thought. "But you can't drive another mile and sleeping in the car again would suck, a bed would be so much better, and we really really won't be any trouble at all, right Lou?"

Lou nodded vigorously. Nate had to agree with them and said finally said so. "That sounds wonderful Mary, if you're sure."

Mary pulled out a Kleenex and sneezed abruptly, shaking her head, then said "OK, it's decided then!"

Elsie spoke up. "Our stuffs in the car, we'll need it."

True enough. The boy had been in long enough to start to warm up a little so he had to steel himself to face another trip outdoors. The girls made it easier, chasing over to get boots and coats back on.

"C'mon Nate, it won't take but a minute."

Lou was standing at the door, ready. Elsie joined her and out the door they went.

He got out of his seat and dragged his jacket on, slipped into his shoes and stepped outside. The girls already had the rear door open, grabbing their stuff. He walked around to the other side and got in the front passenger seat, sitting with his legs outside the car.

The girls were done, had closed the back doors and headed back to the motor home. He reached back and pulled his backpack from the rear seat, setting it on his lap. He popped open the glove box and retrieved the pistol and magazines, and slipped them into his pack.

"What are you DOING?" Elsie was at his door, watching.

"What are YOU doing?"

"I came back for my gloves. Why in the world would you

bring THAT?"

He really didn't know. For some reason he didn't want to leave it in the car, locked or not.

"Shut up, OK?, Don't worry about it, don't even think about it. Grab your stupid gloves and let's get back inside."

She opened the back door as he shut the glove box. Gloves in hand, Elsie hopped back out, and stood, with crossed arms and a frown. Nate pressed the door lock and exited the car.

"What? Don't you be making faces at ME!"

With the bag slung over his shoulder, he grabbed her hand and tugged her back to the meal and rest that awaited them. He opened the door and followed her in.

An incredible smell hit them as they entered. Supper! Nate shrugged off the backpack, and climbed out of his coat and shoes, leaving it all in a pile by the door. A rush of warmth washed over him, with both the furnace and the stove in action.

Mary was at the counter, getting their meal together. Water was set to boil along with that oh so delicious aroma of hamburger frying on a separate burner. Pasta and spaghetti sauce waited on the counter, store bought garlic bread sat in a basket on the table.

Starving, he plopped back into the spot next to Elsie and attacked the bread. It was still warm and unbelievably good.

"Whoa there, save some room for supper! Just kidding Nate, I'm sure you're plenty hungry. Girls, tell Nate what we decided for the sleeping arrangements."

Lou pointed to the rear bedroom. "That's Mary's room. Nate, you'll sleep up there" pointing to the space above the seats in front. "Elsie and I will sleep right here, isn't that cool! The table drops down 'n these seat cushions go on it. A bed!" She thumped the table for emphasis.

Elsie said "That way, you can go to bed and we can stay up later, play cribbage with Mary or something."

Nate nodded approval. Those were fantastic arrangements. That loft looked mighty inviting right now. He could hardly keep his eyes open, and after a bit, laid his arms on the table and plopped his head down. Just for a second he told himself.

They woke him twenty minutes later. It smelled delicious. Spaghetti, cottage cheese and what remained of the garlic bread were served, all washed down with Coke. Nate contributed very little to the mealtime conversation, he mostly focused on eating.

Mary was telling the girls about her life and circumstances.

Widowed, she had traveled around the world with her Air Force husband. They lived in some exotic lands, some pleasant, others not. Six years ago, they returned to the US after his retirement. No children, they couldn't decide on anywhere to settle down and buy a house, so they didn't. The couple hit the road, meeting people, being spontaneous, working thru a succession of motor homes, each one slightly smaller than before, finally settling in this one they were having supper in. Husband, Darrell, had passed away two years ago but she continued their journey solo.

Nate's chin dropped to his chest. The girls snickered as he snapped his bead upright, eyes barely open.

"C'mon Nate, your bed is waiting. Looks like you're ready." Mary got to her feet and offered him an arm. He stood on his own, yawned and stretched. Mary walked over to the door and bent down, headed for his backpack. Nate surprised her as he made a mad dash across the room to scoop it up before she could.

"I'm gonna check out the bathroom first" he said, covering a yawn.

"Sorry Nate, I thought I'd help get your stuff together. That's OK, when you're ready, go on ahead and climb up there." She had another coughing spell, longer that the last one as she shuffled back to sit again.

Nate walked out of the bathroom two minutes later. He mumbled 'g'nite' and waved to the ladies . Lou was looking at him a little funny, Elsie had a frown again.

"Nite Nate." "Nite!" Mary had a "goodnight" for him too.

He threw his backpack up and climbed in behind it. He could barely sit upright but he managed to close the curtains and climb out of his jeans. He wiggled under blanket and sheet. Clean sheets, a great pillow; he was in heaven. The female voices floated at the edge of his awareness, barely, briefly, blurring until he was sound asleep.

CHAPTER SIXTEEN
CONVOY

Blackie slept, or rather crashed, after he pounded down two Bloody Marys shortly after boarding. He woke to the thump of the wheels touching down. It took a minute to get oriented; inside a plane, must be landing in Vegas, yeah the whole situation came flooding back in. Ya made it Blackie. Finally.

His head hurt. Between the pressurized cabin and the booze, he needed aspirins. Oh yeah, plus the police brutality. Exiting was a breeze when you sit in first class; he was in the terminal within 6 minutes of the plane's arrival at the gate.

He went into the closest bathroom to take a piss and retrieve the meds from his backpack, downing them at a water fountain outside the door.

A makeshift plan had formed when he first decided to come out here. Get a car and get a room, at least for the first night. He kept thinking he'd be getting a call, any second now, which would determine his next move. Blackie pulled the phone out of his jacket to check again; no missed calls. The kid had been gone for about thirty six hours now. That's easily enough time to get to Denver or even almost here, assuming driving straight thru.

Was Nate trying that, driving straight thru, not stopping or sleeping? He didn't think so, didn't think that was even possible for the kid. That was time enough for a LOT of things to have happened, many or even most of which would have triggered a call. So that meant he hasn't messed up yet, or maybe did mess up but hasn't been found...

No sense dwelling on that.

The concourse was packed with people, lots of them wearing cowboy hats and boots. He walked by displays showcasing the talent in town at the various big hotels, almost all country acts. Finally, the mystery was solved when he read a display welcoming all the rodeo fans to Vegas for the National Finals. Was that a sign or a coincidence, him there to rope in a runaway.

He walked to the car rental area and made arrangements at Enterprise that put him in an Escape; nice smaller sized SUV. The vehicle awaited just outside the counter doors. The dry fifty degree desert air carried the unmistakable smell and sounds of an airport.

After he stowed his gear in the silver Ford and pulled onto the main drag, he couldn't help congratulating himself for passing thru an airport and not triggering a security incident. Things were looking up.

Blackie had been to Vegas several times, stayed at big places on the strip and smaller ones downtown. He decided to get a room at the Rio Suites, just off the main drag. He'd eaten there the last time, what, 5 years ago, when he was in town on a business trip. It was a little quieter and off the beaten path.

Check in was a breeze; he asked for a room on an upper floor and got one on the 21st. Nice view of the dazzling lights. A fantastic showerhead gave his still aching muscles a hot water workout and washed away the stink of his airport fiasco. Afterwards he went down to have supper at the buffet. Spendy but very good.

He wandered thru the casino on his way back to the elevator, the various slots and card tables filled with gamblers, many wearing western gear. A machine right next to him burst into lights and started a raucous noise; the white-haired woman playing it jumped up shrieking "I Won, I won, can you believe it I WON!" She was quickly surrounded by a crowd, eager to be a part of her good fortune. Blackie thought about going over, shaking her hand, maybe having some of her good luck rub off.

But he didn't. Gambling seemed stupid, luck was something you made for yourself.

He made his way upstairs to his suite. Even though he'd slept on the plane, the big supper was making him very tired. He decided to call Sam before going to bed, let her know he'd made it, seeing if she'd heard anything, maybe see about getting together with her and her mother tomorrow.

The girl didn't answer.

"Sam, this is Angus, Nate's dad. I ah, I made it here, to Vegas and I'm staying at the Rio. Just checking to see if ah, if Nate has contacted you at all, and maybe we could, you and your Mom could have, maybe lunch with me tomorrow? Give me a call. Thanks Sam."

He got comfortable on the bed and flipped on the TV. Local new was all about the rodeo finals and a couple of fatal accidents. Nothing really that interested him. He flipped it off and slid under the covers, wondering once again where Nate was and what was he doing...

##

8:30 AM. Sunday. The sun streamed thru the narrow loft windows, right in Nate's face. He rolled over. Voices were murmuring below, it sounded like the sisters were talking softly in their little nook. He had to pee.

He maneuvered around getting his jeans back on, then lightly jumped down onto the floor. The sisters were lying there, awake, listening to him.

"Morning girls."

"Morning Nate." "Good morning."

He walked thru the motor home to the bathroom and took care of his needs. When he came out, the girls were up, struggling to convert their bed back into a dining area. Nate helped them latch the table top in place, just as a bout of coughing preceded Mary's arrival from her bedroom.

"Good MORNING children! Did everyone sleep OK?"

"Oh yes!"

"Very well."

"Yes, thanks and good morning to you!"

Mary took her turn in the bathroom, returning to her bedroom to get dressed. The two sisters cycled thru too, until finally everyone was back at the dinette.

"Will you three stay for breakfast this fine morning, rest a bit before getting back on the road?"

They all nodded, breakfast sounded swell.

"Lou, can you get the eggs out of the fridge for me, and get the butter too?" Lou got up to help.

Mary was pulling out a fry pan and shortening, getting things situated on the stove. Both girls helped put the meal together, bacon, eggs and toast. After eating, they remained at the table, when Mary launched into what was on her mind.

"I was thinking last night kids, about your situation. Or what little I know of it." She turned to look at the two oldest then sniffed and muffled a cough.

"You say you're going to Spanish Fork Utah, to your Aunt's house. Well I was going to stay on 80 and go to Reno but I'm a little worried about that car of yours, just a little. And I'm not on any kind of schedule or anything and I don't know, I'd just feel a lot better if I maybe took a little detour, made sure you kids made it OK to your Aunt's house. If that's OK?"

She paused. Nate and Elsie looked at each other, Lou looked at her sister. They were caught off guard, didn't know what to say.

Mary continued "I don't want to be creepy or whatever you kids call it these days. I just have a feeling that you maybe need some help."

She paused

"Because it's kind of a weird, or oh, not weird but UNUSUAL for three kids to be on the Interstate all alone, no parents.." She looked at the two oldest kids again.

"And no one ever did say what your parent are doing, where they are..." She waited for an answer.

"Um" Nate looked at Elsie; no help there. He felt he had to keep talking now, was surprised when words kept coming out.

"My Dad, OUR Dad sent us ahead. He had to stay behind, to ah.."

"Dad had to stay back with Mom, she's sick." Elsie said haltingly. "Mom has some problems that are, well are getting worse ya know, so they want us to go stay with our Aunt. For a while, 'til Mom gets better."

All three kids avoided looking at Mary, kept their eyes on the tabletop. Silence.

Mary pondered that explanation; embarrassment, shame? It sounded fishy but she decided not to press it right then. It appeared that all three kids were going to stick with that vague story, and they wanted her to buy it.

"Well then I'm sorry about your Mom's troubles. I don't mean to pry into family business; you just seem to be awful young to be taking on a trip like this. Kids driving cross country, in a car that may or may not make it. How're y'all fixed for money Nate?"

The boy blushed, looked away.

"I'm sorry, there I go, asking rude questions. It's none of my business, just forget I said anything…"

Lou pulled the bills out of her pocket and spread them on the table. "I don't think we have enough Mary. $47."

Nate flared up.

"Lou! Geez, that was for US to know. That isn't Mary's problem, it's OUR problem. WE'LL figure something out OK?"

Nate felt like an ass, raising his voice against Lou like that. But he was worried that Mary was finding out more and more about them. Too much. He wasn't willing to take the risk of trusting her, not yet. How she'd react if or WHEN she discovered the real situation was unknown.

He stood up and tried to look Mary in the eye, avoiding Lou, whose bottom lip was quivering. The senior citizen returned his steady gaze. His guilt forced him to look away, exposed as a jerk with that outburst, embarrassed at the money bind he put them in, afraid he looked like a failure in the eyes of the three females.

Upset with himself, Nate moved to the loft and fumbled with his backpack, waiting to see how this would turn out. Mary spoke next.

"I apologize, Nate's right. That's none of my business, forget I asked. But, that's even more reason for me to tag along. Tell you what, I'll bankroll the rest of the trip; gas, food, my treat! Another night's lodging too, if needed."

"It'll be fun to have some company, real fun. We'll stay together on the road, make what they call a convoy, and if one of you girls would want to ride in here with me, well I'd be tickled pink!"

Nate paused, processing her offer. It was really a no-brainer. He.. THEY sure as hell couldn't say no to that. The boy felt a huge burden vanish, two actually. The lack of money PLUS the fresh nightmare of their broke-ass Cutlass. BOOM. Dealt with.

This of course meant close contact with the woman, the potential for a slipup from the girls or himself, their runaway/stolen car status revealed. It was a challenge but they had her fooled so far, they could keep it up. The alternative was a terrible risk, almost certain to fail.

She seemed cool enough. He got a vibe when they locked eyes a minute ago that he could trust her. He closed his backpack and turned to face her, her and the girls.

Elsie was as relieved as the boy, he could tell. She'd been worried about how they could possibly keep going, how to get from HERE to Utah, specifically. Lou's feelings had been hurt by Nate's sharp tone, but she was out of line, a little.

But it's turning out awesome! Look at the help Mary is offering, this is the BEST possible outcome.

Mary continued. "I have to say, if anyone out here could use a guardian angel, it's gotta be you three. And I would be just worried SICK if I didn't help, knowing the situation you're in, no money, your car and all. So let me be your angel, just to Spanish Fork. Get you delivered safe and sound to your Aunt." She turned to look at Nate.

His relief was evident both in his tone and his expression.

"Thanks Mary, that's really generous. We were getting a little worried, things were looking kinda tough but it isn't like we got NO money, we got ya know, the $47 bucks and all, and.."

He got cut off.

"YES, thank you thank you thank you Mary, you ARE an angel!" Elsie couldn't help it, she jumped up and hugged Mary, bouncing up and down with relief. Lou joined; she had been beyond worried when the car trouble started. The sisters and Mary waved Nate over. "Group hug, group hug!"

The boy laughed and joined them, making it official. They were a team now, heading West. Both the headcount and the vehicle count increased by one.

Mary savored the moment, physical contact being a rarity for her. And with girls, young and full of energy, it was especially nice. This would be a welcome change in her routine, a chance to do some good.

"Come on, we're burning daylight kids. Nate, let's go check the dipstick again, check the anitfreeze. If those look ok, let's get this show on the road."

Nate walked over and grabbed his backpack from the loft, unnoticed. At the door, he shrugged into his shoes and jacket and went back outside. The sky was clear with abundant sunshine, the winds were light. He walked around the RV to the car and opened the driver's door. The backpack got tossed in the back, then he popped the hood release. He heard the motorhome door open and saw Mary come out to join him. She slid her hand into the gap and unlatched the hood. Nate pulled the dipstick, which they both examined closely. A single mark under full. Mary confirmed his thoughts, that was good, for now. He replaced the dipstick and watched as she opened the coolant reservoir cap. It was bone dry.

Mary sent him back to the truck stop with a twenty, to get both another quart of oil and some pre-mixed antifreeze. She waited back inside the RV, chatting with the girls who were delighted that each of them could take turns riding shotgun. Elsie decided to be with Nate now, which suited Lou and Mary just fine. They poured over the atlas, planning a suitable waypoint for the next break.

"It'd be handy to exchange phone numbers, so we can talk between us on the highway." That caught Elsie off guard.

"Ah, we don't have phones Mary. Lou and me. I dunno if Nate does, maybe, maybe its broke or something. He hasn't used it." She almost said 'since we've been with him' but caught herself.

"Really! You don't know if your big brother has a cell phone or not? None of you has a cell phone? How could your

Dad send you out on the highway without a working phone Elsie? That's just crazy." The woman shook her head in disbelief.

Elsie just shrugged. "It's not a big deal Mary."

Stranger and stranger. No phone, teenagers without a phone, not a big deal, yeah right.

"Well I think it's really strange, and DUMB. Out on the Interstate. Here, I'll give you $50, go up to the truck stop and buy a phone, get some minutes. We aren't going to get separated or lost or anything and not be able to talk to each other. Go on, scoot!"

"I'll go too" Lou jumped up and followed her sister to the door. Elsie paused, then returned to Mary's side and bent down to whisper in her ear.

Mary laughed and said "Yes, you girls get any personal needs taken care of too." and peeled off another twenty for Elsie.

Mary stood up, instantly feeling a little light headed. She waved them to the door, announced she was going to lay down, wait for all three of them to return, knock on her door when they're ready. A trail of 'Thanks Mary!' then they were gone.

Darn chest cold, it was getting worse. She shuffled into the bedroom and lay down, piling several comforters on top...

couldn't shake these chills. A couple minutes, quick little nap, she'd feel much better, ready to hit the road again. And she'd have an eleven-year-old for company, won't that be nice.

CHAPTER SEVENTEEN
BUMPER CARS

Angus didn't sleep worth a darn. The bed was comfortable enough, he was tired enough, but his dreams were disturbingly intense. He kept jerking awake as some calamity or another was about to befall him in sleep-world. Dragons, Nate in peril, insurmountable odds holding him back. Very bleak, doom and despair, waking up was truly a relief. He sat up and took a moment to push those emotions away, move into the real world. Or as real as possible in Las Vegas. Rising to his feet, he stretched, still feeling the bruises from yesterday's 'airport incident'. Really tired. Need coffee.

He hit the bathroom, showered, dressed, and left his room, heading down to get breakfast. The buffet was across the cavernous slots area from the elevator. The noise and lights were a tough way to start his day after a poor night's rest.

He went thru the line, loading up on sausage, bacon, hash browns, juice and coffee. Blackie flopped into a booth and started with orange juice and coffee, drinking both before starting to eat. A beautiful waitress kept his coffee refilled as he worked his way thru the meat and potatoes. He watched the people around him, the ebb and flow of casino action, here and there a nest egg or mortgage lost, or a brief winning streak, apparent in the faces. A lot of tired faces, like his own.

A second plate of food was out of the question, he had things to do. He checked his phone; no messages. Time to get busy and start taking care of things now that he's on the ground in Vegas. First up, Sam and her mother.

He left a $5 tip, exited the buffet and headed for the back parking lot and his rental. As he slid behind the wheel, he took a moment to savor the desert climate; sixty degrees was pretty nice in December. Shirt sleeve weather, ride with the window down weather. The forecast back home was for fifteen degrees and light flurries. Between here and there, a big winter storm.

Again he thought of what Nate was doing at this exact moment, and where he could be. Not knowing was stressing him out, his guts were churning. The morning coffee was burning, that damn ulcer. The bad news was, he couldn't do anything til the boy surfaced, in one of many possible ways. God, David Wetterling popped into his head, kid was kidnapped in MN by stranger danger and not located for 30 years. Ack, no, that's not in the cards, not for him and Nate. He was sure of something turning up, they'd be reunited, this wasn't going to go all horrific and worst case. He had to be ready when it happened. He felt being out here put him in the right place at the right time, good news was coming. A silent prayer went up for that outcome, please please.

Blackie felt drained. He just sat there. He had to get his game face on, be prepped to meet the girl and her Mom. Hard to tell what kind of reaction he'll receive, from their perspective he was kinda the cause of this whole fiasco. He decided to not be all woe is me, I'm the victim, my car got stole, even tho that's 100% true. He needed to project confidence, this was all going to turn out OK, Dad is on the scene, has things under control and is ready to leap into action at the first hint of, of, well, anything.

He dialed Sam's number, it went to voice mail. "Sam this is Angus. I'm in town and I'm on my way over to see you and your Mom. Should be there in 20 minutes or so."

Game face ON, go get 'em Blackie. He punched in their address on his phone and wheeled out of the lot.

##

Sam listened to his message with a mix of dread and relief. She was worried sick about Nate, her Mom was too. The whole ticket thing was such a bummer, TOTALLY Angus' fault, such a screw-up, forcing Nate to drive. That's so wrong.

But not knowing was terrible. Two days and no call or text. With Nate's Dad here, that meant he hasn't been in an accident or caught by the cops. And she thought Angus will take some sort of action, not just sit around waiting, or at least she hoped.

"Mom! Mr. MacDonald's on his way over!"

She was yelling into the 3rd floor condo from their courtyard balcony. A freeway three blocks away provided a background buzz that Sam still couldn't tune out. "MOM!"

"Yes, I heard you. Did he say if he has any news?"

Colleen stepped onto the balcony, joining her daughter at the small table after setting down a pair of cold bottled waters.

"No, he didn't mention any. This whole thing is so messed up Mom, and his fault! I'm pissed. And scared; what's going ON with Nate?"

"He's OUT there, somewhere. We're all waiting to hear, from him or about him, or yeah, probably have him show up here honey. Waiting is really hard, but he must be OK, that's the way I'm gonna think. Gonna choose to be positive."

"Well I blame his Dad. None of this woulda happened except for him, That was mean, just dirty, stealing the ticket."

Colleen reached over and patted Sam's arm. "Yes, that wasn't right. But.."

"But nothing! Geez Mom, how can you NOT blame him!"

"I'm sure Angus had no idea Nate would steal his car Sam. That was all Nate's doing, I mean, as a parent, I can see how a plane ticket showing up is, kinda, well, unexpected honey. Puts the parent in a spot, sorta. This coulda been handled better by Angus for sure and maybe by Nate too. Maybe us too. What I'm saying is we can't go back and change what's already happened, we just can't. The important thing is Nate showing up safe. Right?"

Sam sighed. "Yeah. But this waiting sucks. Two days and no news. It can't be much longer, can it?"

Colleen's turn to sigh. She didn't want to acknowledge the possibility that it could indeed take forever for closure, as in a few famous missing person/runaway cases. Bad things happen in the real world.

"Stay positive Sam, think positive thoughts. We'll find out something soon, I'm sure."

A knock! Surely ONE of the MacDonald men.

It turned out to be Angus, a disappointment to the women. He was still welcomed at the door, introductions were made and he joined them on the balcony.

Colleen got to the point.

"No word yet Mr. MacDonald?"

"Please, call me Angus. No, nothing from law enforcement, nothing from Verizon about Nate's phone. I'm very, well I'm both surprised and I guess relieved. No news means no bad news. I mean it's possible that he could show up here. Somehow..." Blackie paused to glance up and down the parking lot, as if the missing Cutlass might magically appear "but it's a long way for even a good driver and I'm pretty sure Nate's driving skills are... crappy. I mean, to be frank."

Sam and Colleen exchanged glances.

"Well, yeah, it's good he hasn't been pulled over or nothing yet, nothing involving the cops. But TWO days?" Sam was just getting started.

"AND he didn't NEED to drive! He coulda FLOWN, he'd already BE here. Instead you, you.." Tears started to flow.

Colleen made soothing noises, patting her daughter's arm.

It was awkward to say the least. Blackie hadn't been in contact with a sobbing female for a very long time. He remained quiet, and stared down at his clenched hands for the half minute it took for the teen to regain her composure.

Colleen broke the silence.

"So is there any sort of plan Angus? Are you going to just hang out here? Well, not here..." sweeping her arm across their rooms "but in Vegas?"

"Yeah, that's a good question. I guess I'm open to suggestions. I only thought it through to the point getting out HERE..."

He waved his arm across the parking lot and out to greater Las Vegas in general

"and believe me, just getting here was something, ah, out of the ordinary let's say. So yeah, I thought I'd touch base with you, see if maybe Nate tried to contact you, then ah, wait thru today maybe, see if the cops turn up anything, if Verizon calls. Just kinda taking it one day at a time, just winging it sorta as stuff happens. I'm just so worried and want things to turn out OK, ya know? So, yeah, not much of an answer, sorry."

Sam piped up. "Waiting sucks!"

Blackie asked "Then you haven't heard from Nate? Nothing at all?"

"We texted Wednesday night, before he left, like I told you when you called. He just said I'd be seeing him. Nothing since then. Waiting sucks!"

Colleen got up and went inside, returning with a US atlas.

"We've been looking at this, wondering which way he'd come."

She plopped it down on the table facing Angus. She leaned over and pointed to I-80. "I think this would be the way to come, taking Interstates. Two days, depending on how much he drove each day, and when he drove.."

"And the weather. There's been a fair amount of snow and wind between Minnesota and here the last two days. I've been watching the radar. There's a blizzard forming here.." Angus brushed his hand from Utah to North Dakota.

"I don't know his plan, how he'd decide which way to go but yeah, I think 80 is a good guess. So if he could drive, I don't know, four or five hundred miles a day, that'd put him.."

He patted the map "somewhere maybe West of Cheyenne. Maybe. And if he did six hundred, oh, maybe close to Salt Lake."

They all stared at the map and considered the implications. Nate probably wasn't going to step thru the door in the next hour, or maybe even the next day if that's about how far he'd gotten. And if the weather was bad, the roads were crappy, he could still be in Nebraska for all they knew. Which boiled down to nothing, they simply didn't know anything. Which made Blackie's plan sound maybe better than it did at first.

Waiting did suck. Blackie offered to take them out for lunch, which was accepted. Colleen suggested a guided tour around Vegas afterwards, get him oriented to the Metro a little, since he may be spending a day or two or more there. Off they went, grateful to have a reason to get out, a destination, a purpose for at least part of the day ahead.

It was 5 hours later, after a big lunch and a tour of the Strip. They'd swung West around the city, gone thru scenic Red Rock Canyon, over east past Nellis Air Force Base. They were headed back, thru North Las Vegas with Sam at the wheel of their leased Ford sport utility. She chauffeured her Mom at every opportunity, having gotten her license a month earlier. Colleen rode up front and pointed out the landmarks to Blackie in the seat behind the teen.

The air conditioner worked to maintain a comfortable temp inside the black vehicle. Angus was nodding off a bit; he blamed it on the beers at lunch. Colleen turned her head around the seat, to look at him. "Did you answer Angus? My question, about going back to our place now?"

He popped his eyes open, focusing on Colleen's face between the seats, replaying her words. Processing an answer, yeah, yeah, back to your place... He'd just opened his mouth to reply when suddenly Sam locked up the brakes, pitching them forward violently. The tires screamed, the truck started sliding a little to the right. Blackie's gaze moved from Colleen to the area ahead of them through the windshield. An area brightly filled with the red lights of a stationary pickup. They didn't stand a chance of avoiding a sickening collision.

Time slowed down as did the three of them, until finally everything crashed with some considerable force into the Ford's bumper. The air bags went off, the lights went out, and Sam, Colleen and Blackie went dark.

CHAPTER EIGHTEEN
GREAT BALLS 'O FIRE

Nate met the sisters as he was returning from the main building. Elsie told him about their mission to get a cell phone which led to a discussion on how that topic came up. He detoured to join them, heading back into the truck stop once again. The boy realized how lame that story must have sounded and told them so but the girls insisted that she bought it completely, wasn't suspicious at all.

Right before they stepped thru the doors, Lou mentioned that Mary went to lay down in the RV while they were gone. Nate thought that was odd; didn't we all just get up? Elsie spotted the display case with the disposable phones in it and soon the three of them were discussing the pros and cons of various offerings.

After securing a consensus, with the cheap Samsung phone activated and in Elsie's possession, she told Nate to wait by the door. The sisters went back to the clothing area and picked up several items, returning to the counter to pay. He caught a glimpse of packages of underclothes and decided to wait outside, blushing as he exited.

The kids walked back thru the parking lot to the two

vehicles. As the girls entered the RV, Nate headed to the Cutlass, and set about getting the coolant added. He was putting the cap back on when Lou stepped to his side.

"Mary isn't feeling well Nate."

Nate looked at the girl and then glanced at the RV.

"What do you mean? What makes you say THAT?" He slammed the hood down and looked at the girl.

"She's coughing and coughing Nate. We couldn't hardly wake her up! I'm worried, Elsie is too!"

Nate didn't need that right now. He leaned on the car, worried about the relative health of their wheels and added to it, fresh concerns about a sick stranger that was their new traveling companion. And benefactor. It occurred to him that what if HE got sick! The girls; the trip could continue if one or both of them came down with that crud but he was a primary driver!

Just then, the starter of the RV cranked over, the engine quickly caught and settled into a fast idle. Mary was up, was ready to go somehow! A miracle. She gave them a thumbs up from the front seat. Lou waved back and dashed inside, throwing a "Hurry Nate!" behind her.

He needed to get the car started, let it warm up while he

pow-wowed with the lady folk, to work out the details of this convoy arrangement. Check on Mary too.

The boy got in the car and sat there. A silent wish was sent skyward for the stupid car problems to magically disappear. If not that, at least let it start right then. The mighty Olds came through, did fire up when called upon. Check Engine greeted him but no others.

The motor did rattle, somewhat from the cold but also evidence that the damage was permanent. Twenty seconds later, the lifter noise lessened as the oil began to circulate. He looked at the cloud of exhaust, white with the cold, not oily blue. Not obviously anyway. He flipped the controls to max defrost and stepped out into the cold Wyoming morning weather.

Traffic was heavy, with cars gassing up and/or taking dining/shopping/bathroom breaks at the main building. In addition, semi-trucks moved thru their own pump islands and parking areas. The section they were in had some occasional activity but not much. He crossed over to the RV and stepped inside.

Mary and the sisters were seated at the table, talking quietly. The new phone was between them, charging off a wall outlet. Nate thought Mary wan't fine, looked a little pale. He thought she appeared worse she did eighteen hours earlier, when they first met, 100 yards away. He didn't plan on staying in very long but took off his jacket and boots anyway. He joined them, standing in his stocking feet looking down on the women.

Mary spoke first. "We don't have a car charger for this phone, just the wall one. It's pretty dead. Elsie and I were thinking, we'll keep this phone here, charging, at least for this morning."

"Mary will let us take her phone in the car Nate. That's OK isn't it"? Elsie continued. "Probably won't even use it.."

Nate shrugged, "Yeah, sure, doesn't matter. More importantly, how you doing Mary? You OK, with the coughing and all. You OK to do this? Really OK?"

She wasn't. Not really. She could tell this was more than just a cold. But she wasn't going to let these kids down, somehow she'd push thru it. She'll take her meds, keep hydrated, probably need to take extra breaks and hop from rest stop to rest stop but for right now she'll fake it. "Smoker's cough kid, heck yeah, I'm OK. Are you?"

That's exactly what Nate wanted to hear but he had to

believe his own eyes, Mary was a wreck. He didn't believe she was a smoker, but whatever. He pushed on.

"What are you thinking, how should we do this? You gonna lead or do you want me in front?"

"Well, yes, to start with, let's do that. You first. We can change later maybe. I think we want to be sure the oil and coolant are going to stay put, so yeah, I'll follow you. For now. Elsie, Lou, what looks like a checkpoint, maybe what, two hours down the road?" She put a fist to her mouth and muffled a slight cough.

Lou pulled the atlas up and glanced at it briefly; she'd already knew where they should stop. "Rest stop, Fort Steele, seventy miles or so West of Laramie. Or else, there's a little town, a few miles further, called.."

"Fort Steele. That's perfect" Apparently Nate had strong opinions. No one else did, so after a little shuffling about, Mary and Lou moved into the front captain's chairs and settled in. Nate and Elsie geared up and went out, closing the motor home's door firmly. The boy reached back and gave it two solid raps, thump-thump with his fist.

"What's THAT for?" Elsie had a quizzical look on her face.

"Saw it on TV or something. It means 'Let's Roll!'"

They climbed into the car. With the heater left running, the interior was toasty warm. As Nate buckled in, he eyeballed the gauges. Check Engine still lit but NO Oil light Temp gauge NORMAL. He relayed that to Elsie, joining her in a "WHOOP". Nate eased the Cutlass into drive and slowly proceeded across the five-acre lot, their destination the freeway onramp a quarter mile ahead.

Elsie swiveled around, confirming the motion of Mary's RV trailing them out of the truck stop. The caravan merged onto Westbound Interstate 80, ten car lengths initially separating the pair but the gap narrowed as the motorhome got up to speed. Nate set the cruise for sixty; Mary matched it.

Both girls began fiddling with the respective radios. Both drivers allowed it.

Mary said, "I have some CDs in the cubbyhole Lou"

The girl had been scanning the available AM stations, unimpressed with the limited choices.

"CDs are really old school Mary. No MP3, or Bluetooth?" She opened the cubbyhole and pulled out a stack of discs. "Not that it matters I guess. Hmm, Jerry Lee Lewis, Walter Trout... Kid

Rock... Never heard of any of 'em. What kind of music is this?"

Mary laughed. "Oh a little bit of this 'n that. Most of it has a beat, something to get you going. Just stuff I like... put in Jerry Lee girl. We'll start out with the 'Killer'. He was so so.. BAD!"

She laughed to emphasize BAD!

"Married his first cousin, she was thirteen years old! People thought he was the devil, thought he played the devil's music. Adults thought that, but us kids loved it, we went crazy. Drove the parents crazy too. Yeah, Goodness Gracious Great Balls O' Fire, that's how we'll hit the road!"

Lou popped in the CD and figured out the play button.

The thumping piano chords came pouring out of the speakers. Mary started belting out the chorus and reached over to crank the volume. Lou smiled, it buoyed her heart to see the old woman revisit her youth like this. It DID have an infectious animal beat. She found her head nodding to the tempo.

Elsie's musical selection for the Cutlass was a FM station playing Muse. Nate wasn't familiar the band but quickly became a fan. It was good traveling music. Elsie was tapping her fingers to the rhythm of "Madness". Nate found himself bouncing his head to the infectious Morse Code bass line.

He kept his focus constantly moving, the road ahead, the rearview mirror, the dashboard. Watching the faster-moving traffic pass their little convoy, merge back into his lane and pull away, a vehicle occasionally peeling off onto an exit ramp or joining the flow at an onramp. The boy adjusted his speed accordingly.

The ever-present Winnebago followed at a pretty constant four car length distance. He noted the absence of the red oil light and the needle on his engine temp gauge making tiny changes within a narrow range. Eyes back to the windshield, where the sunlight that had poured into the Cutlass to start the day was now dimmed by a layer of clouds. A cross wind began to send fingers of light snow across the road, picked up from the ditch on the north side.

Elsie turned the volume down as the first song ended.

"So, the rest stop is a couple hours away. That makes Spanish Fork about another 350 miles Nate. What's that, seven or eight hours? We can maybe get there today!"

Nate thought for a minute, yeah. 7, maybe 8 hours. He glanced at the radio; 10:15.

"Yeah, that would be after supper. After dark. If we can

keep up this pace. If."

He turned to look at the girl. Elsie was frowning. He asked "What?"

"So, we roll into town. Then what? How do we hook up with my Aunt? How we gonna find her? And Mary, she'll realize something isn't right, our story stinks. What's she gonna say?"

Nate turned his attention back to the road.

"I don't know Els, I really don't. We've been faking it this far, I guess we keep faking it. I mean, I've just been taking things a step at a time, a mile at a time, geez. Somehow, things just keep working out. Let's get to our rest stop, Fort Cannonball or whatever, see how we're doing then."

"Fort Steele! Duh."

He thought for a minute.

"You're right tho, we gotta track down your Aunt somehow. Search for her; Google her I guess. Can't just drive thru Spanish Fork, asking random strangers if they know... Who exactly are we looking for anyway? And how much do you remember?"

Before Elsie could answer, Nate froze. A Wyoming state trooper was parked on the shoulder just ahead. He didn't have anyone pulled over, the solitary cruiser sat there idling. Nate glanced at his speed; 62. Under the limit; maybe too far under? Maybe suspiciously slow?

The boy didn't turn his head as they flashed by the squad, he kept his focus straight ahead, his motion smooth. He glanced in the rear-view mirror. Mary moved into the left lane before the RV passed the cop, as he should have done, dammit! He switched to the side mirror and watched as the sinister car receded around a curve behind them, out of sight. The motor home returned to the right lane. He breathed a sigh of relief, still watching in the mirror.

"Nate!" Elsie's voice snapped his eyes to the front, to see he'd crossed the center line. The boy jerkily got back where he belonged as he gripped the wheel even tighter. He looked across Elsie and caught sight of the cop car in that mirror, turn signal on, accelerating back onto the Interstate a mile or so behind Mary, just past that curve. Oh CRAP! "The COP, he's coming!"

Elsie spun around to stare out the back. Nate started sweating as his face quickly drained of color. His eyes flicked between the road ahead and the mirrors. Elsie gasped and grabbed his thigh as the office flipped on his lights, picking up speed rapidly, closing the gap to the RV. The boy started to panic. Run for it? Or pull over, meekly submit? His eyes flickered between the road ahead and the mirror's view behind.

The highway patrol veered into the left lane. Nate heard the siren come on. Shitshitshit! He tried to think...

Els squeezed his leg harder and started saying "No no no.." His eyes tracked the squad car as it passed Mary's vehicle, still gaining speed, the wail of the siren growing louder, increasing the tension inside their stolen Cutlass.

As the cop closed the gap, Nate stared straight ahead, a death grip on the wheel. He hissed to Elsie

"Don't LOOK at him AND LET GO OF MY LEG!!"

She jerked her hand away, and swiveled her head to the front, dramatically, obviously. Both occupants held their breath, bodies rigid, hearts racing as the Chrysler 300 came closer, closer and then overtook them in the left lane. Ominously, it slowed down and matched their speed exactly, keeping pace directly alongside them. Nate didn't dare look, he just kept staring straight ahead, looking guilty as hell.

Suddenly the cop slowed sharply and dropped behind the Cutlass, his car executing a hard left, doing a U-turn thru the median. He shifted over to eastbound 80 and disappeared behind them, taking the lights and siren and tension with him.

Elsie swung her head back, pumped with their most excellent good fortune, and grabbed his leg again.

"WOO Doggie!"

Nate physically slumped forward, his muscles (and his sphincter) unclenching. Wow. His hands were slippery with sweat. "Man oh man Elsie, how close was THAT?" She raised a hand, he gave her a high-five and let out a nervous laugh.

"I wasn't worried… much!" She was grinning from ear to ear.

"Well, I was. I just about crapped my pants Elsie."

"Eww, gross!"

He looked in the mirror at the RV behind them. Mary flashed her lights and gave the horn a toot. They were celebrating too.

Several minutes later, a wisp of blue trailed behind the Cutlass. Mary flashed her lights again. Nate scanned the gauges, temp OK, oil light unlit. He thought he heard something tho and listened intently. The phone rang, startling him a little. Before it rang again, he heard it. The soft tick tick sound of the lifters in his engine. Not loud, just barely noticeable, but if you were listening for it, you heard it now. The 2nd ring drowned out the dreaded noise. Elsie answered.

"Hey, did you see that? Wow, that was scary, we both… OK, sure, here he is"

She handed Nate the phone. "It's Mary."

"Nate, I'm seeing smoke out of the exhaust, blue smoke. You're burning oil again."

He didn't want to hear that, they were past that, he'd put a couple quarts in just… fifty miles ago. 50 miles, that's bad. The ticking remained in the background, dim but very menacing.

"Yeah, I see it too. I hear it again too, just a little. The light isn't on yet Mary, so that's good, right?"

"Well yeah, we don't want to see that light so it's good. For now. With the noise back, even a little, it's bad. It'll be worse when it gets louder. That would be after the light comes on, but that's gonna be real bad news Nate."

A brief coughing spell before she could continue.

"Let's keep going, maybe slow down a little, down to 60 or even less. Keep listening; if it gets really loud, banging and clattering, you'll have to pull over fast I guess. If it stays kinda quiet, we'll push on to the rest area, get off, let things cool down, check the dipstick. If we're lucky, we can keep going, keep dumping oil into it every, oh, hundred miles or so. We may limp into Spanish Fork kiddo, but we'll get you to your Aunt's. How's that sound?" She sneezed.

"Yeah, OK Mary, Fort Steele rest area, next stop. Thanks."

He handed the phone back to Elsie who said a couple words before hanging up.

"Mary's cough is getting worse."

No kidding he thought. Another thing to worry about. Stolen car, runaway sisters, cops, a sick engine and now, a sick adult.

Vegas seemed a million miles away right then.

He kept his eyes moving, windshield, mirror, gauges, repeat. The RV kept pace behind them. The gauges remained neutral. But a few snowflakes began blowing across the highway in front of him, doing lazy, swirling patterns on the roadway.

A sign marking the rest stop appeared – two miles! They could make that easy. The dash remained free of additional warning lights, the engine noise remained as a background irritant. The exit came into view thru the thickening snowflakes.

Relief flooded thru the boy as he slowed and flipped his turn signal on. A glance in the rear-view mirror was troubling; the lumbering RV was just barely in sight, even as Nate's speed the last few miles dropped below fifty. Mary wasn't keeping up.

As Nate merged to the right, he slowed even more. A slight incline before the rest area spread out before them. It had a fair number of vehicles scattered about the parking area. He rapidly eyeballed a spot for the two vehicles before the main building and nosed the Cutlass in, almost, sorta close to the curb. There was plenty of space on his left for the RV Elsie was watching intently thru the back window, coaxing their traveling companions to the sanctuary.

"Come on Mary, we made it, you can too!" She turned to look at Nate, panic in her eyes. "She sounded really bad on that call, like really terrible. What if she needs a doctor or something?"

"Let's just get 'em parked, get her tucked in, some meds and tea or something in her. First things first Els, they gotta make it in here!"

He glanced into the mirror and saw the lights of the motorhome at last! Their speed was under thirty, the vehicle swaying as it wandered across the lane, but they kept coming.

Nate turned off the ignition, silencing the engine clatter that had been so troubling. Elsie squirmed around to lean right behind the boys neck, looking out the side window. She could feel the heat radiating off him. He had turned to the left to watch but caught a scent off the girl that momentarily turned his mind to mush. A gust of wind rocked the car, plastering the windows with a sleet snow mix.

Elsie snapped him back with "What if they CAN'T stop, what if they keep going or smash into somebody?"

"Look, they're gonna make it, they're RIGHT THERE. We can see 'em!'" He sounded more confident than he felt. She managed a weak smile, wanting to believe him.

Then she remembered the coughing on the phone. Mary was sick, and getting worse, not better. Worse would be bad. Worse was, in her experience, more likely. Nate popped open his door and jumped out, thinking he could wave his arms or something to help guide them in for a landing. Elsie scrambled outside to join him.

##

Five minutes earlier, inside the motorhome, Mary was

losing it, had been for the last thirty miles. She was steadily, noticeably getting sicker. The coughing spells came more frequently and lasted longer. She was alternately sweating like a butcher, opening the window, venting in the outside air and then 5 miles down the road, she'd start shivering. Then she'd close the window and crank the heat way up. Over and over.

"I'm so sorry honey, flipping back and forth with the heat and all. It's just so… I'm so…"

The coughing started again and continued for a good 30 seconds.

The girl tried to hide her concern. The rapid decline of both Mary's health and her driving was dramatic and frightening.

"We're almost there Mary, hang on Mary, just a little bit farther. You're doing great, you can do this!"

Lou strained to look thru the windshield, trying to spot the car's taillights. She wondered if they had any idea just how bad Mary was; how could they? Mary was dropping further and further behind, her speed now under 40. The wipers were barely keeping up with the increasing snowfall. She couldn't see the Cutlass, which was distressing.

"Aren't we a fine mess girl. I'm sick, that car is sick,

weather's getting terrible, a bunch of runaway kids…"

Lou's face flushed.

"Run – runaways? US?"

The woman leaned forward, focused intently on the road ahead.

"You're a terrible liar Lou, it's plain as the nose on your face. Stay that way, be a crappy liar, it'll make your life easier if you know you need to always tell the truth. Or maybe something that sneaks around the truth a little closer."

Lou couldn't look at Mary.

"I don't know exactly how you three fit together, I really don't. But you're lucky to have such a good sister to look after you like she does."

More coughing. She fiddled with the heater, turned it down while opening the driver's window, blasting in the cold outside air once more. Lou noticed the old woman was sweating again.

"And Nate, the brother or whatever he is, you two are lucky to have run across him. He cares about you girls and that's something special."

After another silent spell that finally ended with a bout of coughing, the rest area sign loomed into view.

"You're right Mary, bout Elsie taking good care of me, of both of us. And we care about Nate too."

She strained to look again for the lights of the Cutlass, to confirm that she wasn't in this alone. It was scary being with the sick old woman.

The RV slowed even more as it came to the exit. Mary flipped the blinker on and moved over to the right, leaving the freeway behind, the destination at hand.

"I'm not doing so good, not good at all Lou."

The old woman glanced at the girl, her face a ghastly shade of gray, eyes and nose running. Before she could turn back, Lou watched her eyes roll up and her lids close. She slumped in the driver's seat, and as she slid against the door, her arm eased the steering wheel to the left.

"MARY!"

The girl froze. Time seemed to slow way down. The vehicle angled to the left, heading off the roadway in slow motion. They were just past the handicapped section of the parking area, Lou saw the Cutlass there, and the teens standing beside it waiting for them. The girl had the presence of mind to grip the wheel and gently turn it back to the right. The Winnebago slowed to a crawl now, moving across several snow-covered parking spaces, headed towards the front of the Cutlass, until gradually the left tire hopped the curb. That ended their slow-motion arrival, slightly off kilter. Lou let out the breath she'd been holding and turned off the ignition.

Mary was crumpled against her door, breathing raggedly, sweating, moaning. Lou pulled her back upright and cradled the woman's head, sobbing.

CHAPTER NINETEEN
EVOLUTION

The noise at first. So loud. Then Blackie was aware of movement, rocking from side to side. He could tell he was in a vehicle. His face hurt like hell.

"Sir, can you hear me?"

He opened his eyes, slowly. His head, his eyes, everything hurt. The light was painfully bright, he had to squint. Focusing was a problem for a minute. He realized the noise was a siren: I'm in an ambulance!

"What happened?" An attempt to sit up failed immediately; he was strapped on a gurney. Tight bands across his chest locked him down. They slowed and then turned a corner, throwing his body to the right, away from the EMT who asked about his hearing. He felt queasy.

"Mr. MacDonald, you were in a car accident. You have lacerations on your face and probably a lot of bruising. We're about seven minutes away from University Medical Center sir. Just lay there for a little while longer, OK?"

Accident? He struggled to remember anything before waking up in here, he wasn't even sure where they were. It was hard to concentrate, with his face throbbing. He felt a migraine coming on, that god damn siren! He moaned.

"Where are we? Where was the accident?"

The EMT leaned towards Blackie.

"Open your eyes wider for me sir, try to focus on my finger please."

It was difficult, his lids didn't want to cooperate, when they finally did, he saw the young attendant holding his index finger in front of Blackie's nose. He began to move it, side to side then up and down.

"Do you know where you are Mr. MacDonald? Do you know what day it is?"

Blackie frowned, didn't reply.

"You were in a crash on Interstate 15. That's in Nevada. Las Vegas to be specific. Do you remember being in Las Vegas today sir, coming to Las Vegas?"

Vegas. Yeah, that sounded vaguely right, something something Vegas. He was pretty sure Vegas isn't home, that didn't feel right... but he suddenly panicked. Where DO I live?? The guy said coming to Vegas, coming from somewhere else, coming from home. He thrashed around a little, his headache growing worse. That siren, he couldn't put two thoughts together, that fucking siren…

"Hang on sir, another couple minutes, stay with me."

But Blackie couldn't hang on and faded out.

##

The motorhome had made it's agonizing stop just inches from the Cutlass, blocking three spaces as it nosed in at an angle. The teens dashed inside to the emotional scene, Lou between the seats holding Mary's head, weeping.

Elsie ran to her little sister, crying herself. "It's OK, you MADE it, you got here and stopped and everything!"

The girls stood, making room for Nate. "Mary, can you hear me, Mary? It's over, you MADE it! Mary?" He maneuvered her upright in the seat and grabbed a bottle of water out of the console. "Mary! Here, take a drink of water, you'll feel better. Mary?"

A brief flutter of eyelids gave them hope. The old woman launched into a coughing spell, more hope. When that died down, she managed to grab the water and took a good pull. Her eyes finally opened and took in the concerned expressions around her.

"Sorry 'bout that you guys. I'm just wiped out I guess."

The boy gently spun the chair to the center and stood ready at her right elbow, Elsie quickly moved to the other side to help.

They let her sit there for a minute, catching her breath. When she was able to keep her eyes opened and focused, she gave the signal to stand.

Nate did most of the boost and Elsie helped her with balance. Lou was wringing her hands, feeling helpless and somehow responsible. Once Mary was upright, a little color returned to her face. She pointed to the dining area and started shuffling over under her own power with Nate and Elsie on either side.

"Lou, would you get the tupperware box of meds out of the bathroom for me honey?"

Lou was back in a flash. Elsie had the water placed on the table as Mary picked thru the bottles. She opened several and retrieved a pill from each, three total. Her hands trembled a little, fussing with the pills and the bottle caps. But she did it herself.

"This cold, it's kicking my butt."

She shivered as she popped the tablets in her mouth and

took a drink to down them. Lou had brought a fleece blanket out and draped over the old woman's shoulders.

"How's the Cutlass boy?"

Nate told her the knocking had returned, louder. She pulled the fleece tighter around her shoulders, then asked him to check the dipstick again.

He was relieved to have something to do. After being gone for a couple minutes, he returned to the camper.

"It just barely shows on the bottom Mary."

She sighed. That's what she feared.

"I think it's the end of the line for your car kids. At that rate, 35 miles to the quart, it's a lost cause."

Her voice was wheezy, her breathing ragged. Within mere moments she threw off the blanket, sweat popping out on her forehead. A couple of short hard coughs then she finished off the opened water.

"So thirsty.. Bring all your stuff over, empty it out. We're gonna keep going OK? Get you to your Aunt, in Utah OK? We'll all ride together in here."

Another brief coughing spell took its toll, she was out of breath.

"I have GOT to lay down. We can all take a break for a couple hours while I catch a nap, or.. or..."

Her voice trailed off. She looked at Nate.

He didn't like that look.

"Or what?"

"I really don't know if I'm up for anymore driving, we can wait and see if I get better, but right now, it doesn't look good. But if you're up for it, maybe, YOU can take the wheel, get us moving towards your Aunt.. If you think you can handle this rig Nate."

"You mean get us moving towards a doctor for YOU!" Elsie knew this was getting serious.

"Well, that maybe isn't a bad idea girl. I don't ever remember feeling this poorly."

She emphasized her comment with another round of coughing.

Nate was apprehensive, he knew it'd be way different to drive the Winnie. He wondered just how HARD it might get. Through the mountain passes. With the worsening snow and wind. This has gotta be a heavy 'ol boat. Way different than the Cutlass.

But, they really didn't have much choice. Mary needed medical attention, they could stay here for a while but if she continued to go downhill, time was a factor.

Mary shakily got to her feet, swaying slightly, croaked out her need to visit the bathroom, then get some sleep. The two girls assisted her back to the bathroom, then tucked her into bed.

Nate went back outside. He made several trips between the vehicles, bringing over the backpacks, blankets and remainder of the car's contents. Taking the keys out for a final time, he locked the door and felt homesick. The Cutlass was his link to the life he left behind, and it was scary leaving it. But he was angry too, the stupid car let him down, bigly.

He returned to the RV and joined the girls at the dinette. Mary was snoring in the bedroom. Nate listened as Lou outlined the distance remaining, just over three hundred miles. It was 3PM. They could get to Spanish Fork yet that day, well night, midnight, if he slid behind the wheel and got them back on the road.

The girls told him it was his decision. They could stay there, see if Mary got better, or heaven forbid, got worse. They could call 911, save her if it came to that. It would doom their journey but that was secondary.

The alternative, the driving burden and stress, the responsibility for all their safety, would fall entirely on Nate. So it boiled down to his decision.

Nate rose, walked up front and wordlessly settled into the driver's chair. He moved it back and forth, up and down, adjusting it to a comfortable position. He swiveled his head and adjusted the side mirrors to get them lined up perfectly. Satisfied, he buckled up and started the engine. Finally, he turned to look back at the sisters.

"I need a co-pilot up here. We also need to start hunting down that Aunt of yours. Use Mary's phone."

He had an expectant look, waiting for a response. The wide smiles on both girls was his answer. Lou stood and grabbed the phone off the counter and handed it to her sister on the bench seat. Elsie nodded and watched Lou plop into the other captain's chair. After getting buckled in, she opened the atlas and then pointed to the right. "That way driver, we are still heading West"

Nate gave her a salute and gingerly slid the vehicle into reverse. He let up on the brake, very conscious of the different sensation of handling this truck. Sitting higher and without a rear-view mirror was a big adjustment. The angle of the crash-landing gave him a perfect view of any incoming traffic as shown in the driver's mirror.

As they crept backwards the tire came off the curb, and they were level again. Backing a little further, he stopped, with the Cutlass outlined in one last view; Lou gave it a sad wave when they lurched forward. The Runaway Express had evolved but was still in motion and still moving Westward.

CHAPTER TWENTY
OW MY HEAD!

Some jackass was sweeping a bright light across his eyelids, first one eye, then the other. As if the siren wasn't bad enough, now light beams were blasting waves of pain into his brain. He raised his arms, tried to shield his eyes as he opened them, was thankful that they'd finally turned off the damn siren.

"There you are sir, can you tell me your name?"

Blackie blinked rapidly, then squinted at his surroundings, moving his head to take it all in.

"Angus MacDonald. Where am I?"

"You're in the UMC ER Mr MacDonald. You were in a car accident. What do you remember?"

"Where? ER, where?"

"Las Vegas sir, the hospital. Are you in pain, does it hurt?"

Hurt? OW, my HEAD, yeah it hurts! Hospital? Vegas? Yeah, Las Vegas, yeah. Nate. It was coming back. He stole my car.

"Ow, yes, I'm in pain, my head" He tried to sit up, got up on one elbow, but that was a killer. Throbbing pain shot across his forehead, a groan escaped. Accident? Me? Was I driving?

He eased flat on his back again, hands covering his eyes.

The sounds of the busy facility washed over him. Voices, machines beeping, movement, a confusing jumble of noise.

Sam! Colleen! The backseat of the SUV, screeching tires and then darkness.

He sat up on one arm again, pried open his eyes a bit, took in the pair of blue scrubs attending him.

"The others, Sam and Colleen, how are they? Where are they?"

"I know two others came in from the same wreck, two females. They're being treated here too. I'll have someone check on their condition sir. If you could lie back, we're going to check your vitals again, then send you down for a MRI. You really banged your head, we need to take a look."

Blackie laid flat again. Pain throbbed behind his closed eyes, in rhythm with his heartbeat. The staff efficiently checked him over, then wheeled him to another room for the promised MRI.

##

The motorhome handled like a slow, lumbering beast compared to the Cutlass. Acceleration was a joke, braking had a totally different feel. Every wind gust moved him, which made staying in his lane a constant challenge. He was barely able to maintain fifty-five; everyone blew by him, many drivers glancing over to check out the bozo crawling along in that underpowered box. His hands held a death-grip on the wheel. It was exhausting for the inexperienced driver.

Lou sensed that. She bent over the open atlas and just started calmly talking.

"This next exit is Hwy 76. To the right. And just beyond that, Hwy 76 to the left. Rawlings WY is a few miles further down the road."

She looked up, checked the view out the windows, glanced at Nate, then continued.

"We're kind of in the high desert. It climbs up and down, but we skipped the real mountains, the Rockies. Skipped 'em so far: they're down in Colorado, south of us. But we'll run into 'em when we get out of Wyoming, we dip down into Utah then."

The pre-teen looked up at the driver again, expecting some kind of reaction. She had an apprehensive, half-smile; he was scowling.

His shoulders were killing him, the muscles all knotted up from stress. Nate was getting the rig up to cruising speed on a long flat straight section.

The boy shook his upper body, convulsively, briefly, then smiled back.

"Grab the wheel for a sec."

She wasn't expecting that. "Huh?"

"C'mon, just put a hand on the steering wheel, gently, OK?"

Lou hesitantly put her left hand lightly on the wheel.

Nate pressed the cruise button, unlatched his seatbelt then suddenly stood up!

A very surprised Lou let out a squeak when he did but managed to keep a steady hand on the wheel; they didn't swerve at all.

The driver stepped behind his seat and stretched way overhead, then bent down and touched his toes. He shrugged out of the hockey hoodie he was wearing and threw it into his overhead loft. Lou kept them in their lane during Nate's six second muscular and mental health break. He finally plopped back into the seat, belted up and reclaimed the wheel. The young navigator received a big smile.

"You're a natural driver Lou, just like me!"

They exchanged a laugh and high fives. Lou bent down to the map again, estimating speed and distance, looking for the next stopping point. She liked to have a plan, have things laid out, know what was happening next. It didn't always work out that way, heck here she is tearing across Wyoming in a stranger's motor home, a sick stranger, driven by another stranger being chased by the cops. At least Elsie was there with her and so far, they were doing pretty darn good.

Nate was slowly getting a feel for driving this unit. As he got five miles experience, the handling got a little more predictable. He'd vary his speed, trying to build it up before climbing a hill because inclines killed his momentum. He backed off the gas as a downhill approached, tried to not ride the brakes. The mostly tail wind helped but it did swirl and catch him sideways occasionally. He learned to watch for close rock walls and quickly opening canyons on his sides, got better at making the necessary adjustments.

Now he was hovering around 50 or slightly faster. The speed limit was 80 and all the other traffic was moving even faster than that. He'd see someone appear in the side mirrors and within a minute or two, they zoomed by. He didn't care. The right lane was all his and he felt safe there.

It felt like the wind was gusting a little more which meant he was fighting the wheel harder. His sore shoulder muscles triggered a memory of Mom.

When he was little and couldn't sleep, Mom would sit on the edge of his bed and talk to him, rub his chest and get him relaxed. She told the boy to turn off his brain and just imagine his body all stretched out. She'd start at the top of his head and have him visualize that body part, have him tense that muscle and then consciously relax it, getting it loose. Then she'd move down, neck, shoulders and arms. Her words and the mental images she conjured up brought him relief.

"Feel your neck honey, those muscles are so tight. Let 'em go loose and soft. They feel good, your neck is smooth now Baby. So easy and light. Drop to your shoulders Nate. First the left one.."

Before the two of them got to his feet and toes, Mom's voice was so quiet, her touch so light, he'd be out.

Thinking of his mother brought a lump to his throat; his eyes teared up. But it was also timely. He needed to shake off this tension.

While maintaining a focus on his driving, Nate walled off a section of consciousness to start at the top of his head, to tighten and then unclench his scalp, and his temples, loosen the muscles, and then moved down to his neck. And from there, to his shoulders and arms. It worked. He rolled his head and shrugged the tightness out of his shoulders, felt refreshed, ready for another hour or so at the wheel.

A glance across the gauges showed all well there, thank god. They had gas, the oil and temps were steady, battery charged.

Without the sun streaming thru the windshield any more, it actually had gotten chilly in the cab. The solid overcast, with fast moving clouds scuttling above them, made it dreary. He reached for the heater control.

"A little cold for ya? I think so…"

"You're the driver, you get comfortable. I'm fine."

Lou had gleaned all the necessary info from the atlas, knew where they were, the route to their destination. She looked out the windshield and watched the scattered traffic, the impact a passing semi had on their vessel and assessed Nate's steady driving improvement as the miles added up.

She turned and called out.

"How's it going back there Els?"

Elsie wasn't very good with cell phones. Mom had one, but it was often out of minutes and certainly wasn't available to her kids. All her school friends had a phone, it was embarrassing to say the least that Elsie didn't. Both friends, two. She felt a pang of loneliness thinking about Omaha, but just a little. They'd never stayed anywhere long enough for her to think of it as 'home'. She was used to being new in school, new apartments and neighborhoods. Inside, she was pretty tough.

The one constant was Lou, and the need to take care of her little sister, because she wasn't tough, not yet. Not like Elsie. To tell the truth, Mom needed looking after too, lately anyway. She was losing it, being in a haze at home most of the time, drunk and high. She wasn't violent, Elsie was thankful for that. Mom would pass out. Mostly in her room, sometimes on the couch, but usually sprawled out on the bed. Lou pretended that she was sick, and Elsie agreed, it was a sickness. So the girls took the EBT card and shopped for groceries. They took turns with cooking, (microwaving), and they got themselves to and from school.

Mom had her good days, a couple a week. Those were

teasers, imitations of normalcy, of family. Those days were cruel because they gave the girls hope that things could stay like that, Mom could get her shit together, that they could be more like the other kids. But true to form, they'd come home the next afternoon or the one after that and find a note on the table.

"Back soon, love Mom".

And it might be soon or it might be a day or two but the next time they saw dear old Mom, she'd be blasted and out of it. That cycle occurred over and over.

Mary's phone was in Elsie's hands; she'd gone back to the bedroom and took it out of the woman's purse next to the bed. She was on her right side, facing Elsie, sleeping, wheezing. Elsie pulled the fleece up over Mary's shoulder then left the room, phone in hand. She didn't close the door; she wanted to be able to hear if Mary called out or got up. Or fell out of bed.

She was back at the table, and had zoned out, thinking of what they'd left behind, when her sister's words snapped her out of those depressing thoughts. She threw on a fake smile and replied "It's going!"

But it wasn't. The phone was locked or something. Elsie was stuck. She didn't know how to unlock it but didn't want to admit that. The screen was dark, remained dark when she stabbed at it with her finger like she'd seen people do. She poked it a couple more times, nothing. She felt like a dummy.

She was about to swallow her pride and ask Lou for help, when a button at the bottom she happened to touch lit up the screen. Wow, REALLY a dummy, duh.

Elsie called out from the dinette.

"Hey guys, I got Mary's phone opened. Annddd...got an alert right away, some weather app. It says... oh no, it says Winter Storm Warning! We're heading into a blizzard!"

##

This was Blackie's first MRI. Hopefully his last. It was an odd experience, wearing earbuds, having to remain motionless for several fifteen-minute sessions inside the intimidating metal tube. The headache diminished, surprisingly, during the procedure. Probably as a result of the pain pill he'd requested after leaving the ER.

The area where he waited following the scan was comfortable. It was OK for him to get off the gurney; he was upright in a padded chair and had a bottle of water at his side. His clothes were in a locker but they'd ask him to not get dressed yet.

He had the small room to himself.

Two medical personnel walked in. The taller one said "Mr. MacDonald, I'm Dr Moore, I've looked at the images."

He had a couple of papers in his hand, glanced at them both again. "We don't see anything to be concerned about in the scans. No swelling, nothing out of the ordinary. Stand up sir, tell us how you feel."

He reached for Blackie's arm, helped him to his feet. Not lightheaded, not dizzy. The doctor asked him to turn in a circle; he rotated 360 and stopped. Still good. He gave the doctor two thumbs up.

"Close your eyes Mr. MacDonald, tilt your head back."

Blackie did.

"Now stretch your arms straight out sir."

Yeah, he could do that too.

"Touch your nose please."

Blackie laughed.

"Gee Doc, I know where this is going. Next it'll be 'walk a straight line' right? Honestly, I wasn't driving, I was in the back seat!"

The doc laughed. "Not a DUI check sir, but close. Humor

me please."

Blackie touched his nose and threw in an exaggerated heel-to-toe motion for 10 feet. They all laughed.

"So, again, how do you feel Angus?"

"Like I was beat up Doc. Sore. Still got a headache too though not as bad as earlier."

"Car accidents will do that. Consider yourself lucky Mr. MacDonald, not everyone is as fortunate"

"No shit Doc. The other two, the women, Sam and Colleen. How are they? They're here right, they're OK?" Blackie shot a silent prayer upwards.

"Well, privacy guidelines don't allow me to discuss the details but yes, they're here. They're being seen, I don't know if they've been admitted. Check at the desk outside"

"Thanks Doc! That's great. Hey, how about me? What am I, er, not admitted? Checked out? What?"

"You sir, are free to go."

Blackie you're one lucky dog; he counted his blessings yet again as he followed them out. He picked up his things from the locker; everything he came in with was there. Keys, wallet, loose change. And his phone. He checked; no calls. No Nate.

After asking at the nurse's station, he located the two women; Colleen had been looked at and released. Sam wasn't as lucky. A broken arm and for a teenaged girl even worse, a prominent black eye. They were in a waiting room outside the ER, marking time until the 'Kast Krew' showed up with splint and plaster for the arm.

The girl was in a degree of pain and wasn't talkative. However, Colleen was all wound up and jabbered a mile a minute. She see-sawed between relief that things weren't worse and panic over Sam's injuries. Blackie's arrival and lack of obvious wounds was quickly processed.

"My GOD, it all happened so FAST! Are you really OK baby? I heard the tires squealing, the CRASH! We coulda all been KILLED, My GOD!"

Blackie endured several minutes of the hysterical monologue and decided his presence was definitely optional.

"Colleen, you stay here, take care of Sam. I'm gonna go pick up my rental from your place, go back to my hotel and take a hot shower ya know? I'm sure things will be fine, your daughter will be OK, I'll check in with you later, OK?"

Collen just nodded and waved her hand at Blackie

dismissing him. She was feeling this was all his fault, the fact that they were even together at that particular time and place. But damn, her daughter was driving, she rear-ended that pickup, the accident was really on her, as much as that sucked

Sitting in the Uber on the way back to the Needles condo, Blackie tried to make sense of things. Where was his son? It was the end of day three for the boy on the run. Was he still in motion, still safe? If not, what could explain the silence? A couple of possibilites quickly popped into his head which he quickly squashed; no downer 'what-ifs' allowed. No news is OK, is GOOD! That would be his mantra.

He needed to get out of his clothes, get his aching muscles in a hot shower and slam some Ibuprofen stat. Maybe some supper too. And then, try to fall asleep, turn off his brain, recharge mentally for whatever tomorrow would bring.

His driver was listening to the radio. "Big storm north of here. Not supposed to reach us thank god, we had one of those last month. Shut down the Strip and everything, it was a real mess for a bit."

Angus groaned, one more thing to worry about. Another wordless prayer sent up for his son's safety, wherever he is -

amen.

CHAPTER TWENTY ONE
FINDING AUNT TRACI

They were OK for the moment. The storm was still ahead of them, the full brunt of the wind and snow yet to be felt. A few flakes skittered across his windshield, the advance scouts. Elsie's announcement of the approaching blizzard made his mouth go dry and his palms sweat. He didn't want to wrestle this motorhome thru any kind of weather, knew they'd have to hunker down soon, ride it out. Lou was on it, atlas open.

"Table Rock Nate. Right on the interstate. 'Bout a hundred miles."

She looked up from the spot on the map her finger marked, Table Rock it said, and looked at the driver. He glanced quickly at Lou, then eyes forward again.

"A hundred miles?" His voice cracked as he said it, bringing an immediate blush to his cheeks.

In a forced, much lower voice he said "Ahem, let's try that again... A hundred miles huh?"

She laughed and replied in an equally absurd low, gravelly voice. "As the crow flies."

That got a thin smile out of him, lifted his dark mood

brought on by the storm warning. He relaxed his hands, one at a time, then did the shoulder roll again.

Elsie had been quiet for too long. Lou stood and told Nate she'd bring him a coke and moved back to the dinette table. The older girl was trying to get to a search engine, get to the browser on Mary's phone. She didn't know where the icon was, the screen had quite a few but none that she recognized. The younger girl saw the struggle and bent down to look at the new phone Mary purchased at the truck stop. She pointed. "Try this one Sis."

"Duh, thanks Lou. Forgot about that one."

The Safari compass needle was prominent on the screen. She got to Bing, and then paused, wondered what to enter for their search terms. She looked up at her sister, hoping for some help.

"Start with Spanish Fork I guess, let's see what that gets us."

Elsie punched it in, got the obligatory hotel ads at the top, a map, the wiki, a city website, realtors, just a lot of stuff. She was overwhelmed with the possibilities and couldn't think of what to do next. She passed the phone over to Lou, a pleading look on her face.

That was fine with Lou, she possessed a logical mind, excelled at puzzles, maps, reading. She flopped down in the seat and curled over the table, phone in her hands, digging in.

"Driver ordered a coke. Maybe something snacky too. Go be his co-pilot Sis, I got this."

Elsie was relieved as she stepped over to the fridge. The swaying vehicle made her reach out to steady herself. A crash sounded, something fell in back. The rocking took a little getting used to, but she made her way towards the rear. Inside the bathroom, a cabinet door was hanging open. A couple of medicine bottles were in the sink; she put them back, latched the door and closed the bathroom up behind her.

Mary's door was partially closed; she rapped on it softly, then let herself in. Mary was sound asleep and had kicked off her covers. Elsie felt her forehead, like she remembered her mother doing. It was damp, cool. Definitely not burning up. The girl figured that was a good sign and quietly slipped back out.

She could tell they had slowed down as she grabbed a couple Cokes from the fridge. A glance showed Lou taking care of business, working the phone, paper and pen in use on the table. Somehow a bag of white cheddar popcorn jumped into Elsie's hands from Mary's cabinet. She made her way up front, offerings in hand.

"Buckle up Els."

The driver looked stressed. She bent down and situated the food and drink. When she took her seat and belted in, a dramatic view opened ahead.

Their long gradual uphill climb was coming to an end as the road turned slightly south. As the truck labored harder and harder getting to the crest, it's speed slowly dropped; down to 40 now.

The snowflakes were getting larger but seemed to have tapered off, more scattered. The wind was worse, it swirled even harder as he rose out of the canyon they'd been in for the last five minutes. The horizon was suddenly visible at the crest. And what a mind-blowing sight spread out before their insignificant little vessel.

A solid line of snow, black in intensity, filled the view ahead, a literal curtain falling across their path. Beautiful sunshine in front with a churning, dark wall behind. A stark contrast between calm and chaos. The boundary was just beyond a small town, which still shone brightly in the sunlight. Nate's mind tried to estimate the distance but drew a total blank. He was struggling with the wheel more and more, fighting it really. The sight of that weather, the thought of what it must be like INSIDE that weather scared the crap out of him.

"Forget a hundred miles, If we're REAL lucky, we'll make it to THAT town, whatever it is. If.."

His voice trailed off.

##

The Uber dropped Blackie off at the Needles condo. Getting behind the wheel of his Escape took a series of painful adjustments as his battered body complained. The drive back to his hotel was thankfully uneventful.

He headed straight to his room, stripped and took a long hot shower. Afterwards he lay on his bed and debated crawling in for a nap or a full night's crash 'n burn. Ow my head, not funny. He closed his eyes, just for a second, and woke up several hours later.

A horizontal inventory yielded the following: head, ow and OW! Shoulders/arms; black and blue. Back and legs: marginal at best. Stomach; empty. Bloodstream alcohol content; also empty. Well he could do something about the latter two.

After dressing, he popped a couple Tylenol and made his way down to a casual dining room. It was his lucky day after all; early bird special on prime rib and baked potato. He got a booth and after ordering it and a beer, popped open his phone. No calls, what a disappointment. He couldn't help but wonder again, where was Nate right NOW, where he was and how he was. The not knowing was a grind, as difficult to deal with as his battered body.

He drew a blank on useful calls to make as he stared at the phone so he opened a browser to a news site.

Big storm. Top story, a fast-moving clipper bearing down from the northwest, gonna miss Vegas and brush Salt Lake, taking dead aim at Denver. Damn Nate, I hope nothing's happened to you, that you're still safe and if on the road, taking it nice and slow. Hunker down Son, ride out that storm somewhere. Call for help.

He shook his head, sent another prayer skyward, and ate his meal when it arrived. He didn't enjoy it, couldn't quit worrying about his boy out there. Blackie felt down, way down, physically and emotionally. Drained, beaten, almost out of hope. He paid and left, unaware of the noisy flashy slots that he passed on his way back to the elevators. 8 hours of oblivion beckoned sweetly. It was 7:30PM.

##

Rawlins Wyoming Welcomes You! The sign plainly said so, off to the right. Barely visible thru the shrieking horizontal snow. Another sign. KOA. The boy had slowed to thirty, was just limping along, hoping to get off on the next exit and park this sucker.

His nerves were shot, his hands were rigid claws from a death grip on the wheel, his arms ached after fighting the gusts that battered them. Visibility extended to the blinking taillights of a semi immediately in front of him, who in turn was tight on the rear of another big rig. Leading the convoy was an immense Wyoming DOT snow plow, blazing a trail.

The girls had rotated thru the other seat. Two minutes earlier, the doors behind them opened and closed; Mary was up. She finished in the bathroom and came forward. Her presence was a boost for the beleaguered driver. She bent down to take in the situation.

"You're doing fine Nate, Stay right with this group til the next exit. What's up ahead and how far Lou?"

"About a mile to the Business 80 Loop... that's into town. A Walmart and some hotels. If we stay on the Interstate, there's a truck stop, like two miles Mary. And geez, its GREAT to see you!"

"Thanks Lou, I think my meds kicked in, a little. Town might be plugged up boy. Let's go for the truck stop instead OK? Easy on, easy off. A safe harbor for us, we'll get some supper and wait this nasty old storm out. You can do another couple miles can't ya?"

Elsie rose from the co-pilot chair.

"Here Mary, I'm sure you'll be a lot more help up here than me, sit, sit."

The offer was accepted. Mary took a minute to catch her breath and get oriented.

"It sure looks different sitting over here driver."

Nate took his eyes off the road ahead and shot the older woman a half-smile. She directed him to stay put as they passed by the double lanes branching into the business loop, still following the big trucks. The plow peeled off onto the exit without them. He felt a pang of unease watching it go, it took an improved road surface away with it.

The traffic was sufficient to at least keep tracks open in one lane. Bright lights on the right, off the exit they just left behind.

Mary spoke up.

"That'd be Wal-Mart. Coulda tried to get in there, that might have been OK. But truck stops have more traffic, I think maybe be plowed a little better."

A couple more tense minutes in the right lane, then lights up ahead, on their left. Their destination. She pointed out the exit ramp to the truckstop; a road at the bottom led to an overpass to the truckstop on their left. At the bottom of the ramp, the left turn lane was pretty deep with snow. Nate moved over to make the turn and let his speed drop.

"No no no! Don't slow down!"

Oh my gosh, she didn't want to get stuck at this intersection, not with safety so close. She checked for traffic and then urged him on.

"Go Nate go, keep moving, turn into that clear section, c'mon baby!" The back tires had lost their grip and started to spin. One front tire finally quit plowing snow and got into a open area, allowing their forward momentum to pick back up.

"C'mon BABY!"

All four of them focused their willpower on moving the Winnie forward, up and over to the beckoning truck stop.

It worked! The boy feathered the throttle and picked his path carefully. He negotiated the turn onto South Higley Blvd and the well-lit Rawlins Travel Center complex was right there! They crossed over the interstate bridge and made it!

He turned in and kept to the right, and at Mary's direction, angled over to a spot under the tall lights illuminating the North end of the lot. They were separated from the main building by four hundred feet of snow-covered tractor-trailers.

"We'll be out of the way for them to plow but easy enough to get ourselves out." She said, nodding approvingly.

Nate angled them into the position she wanted, with the wind at their back. Drifts will form in front, our rear tires will be clear. We'll back out she said.

He took one last look at the dash then flipped off the outside lights and switched off the key. The only sound breaking the silence was the wind, the motorhome gently rocking in rhythm to it's changing direction. The relief was immense.

Elsie started it. A slow clap clap clap. Lou nodded and

joined in, then Mary, the three of them clapping together, smiling, chanting "Nate Nate Nate!"

He rose from his seat, arms clasped together overhead, giving the Rocky pumping move. The happy moment ended with a coughing spell from Mary, not as bad as some earlier ones but still bad. It finally wound down, with ragged breathing and obvious exhaustion showing on her face. She rose and moved to the back.

"You kids round up something to eat, get settled in for the night. I need some more meds, need to lay down again. See if I can't beat this thing. I'll get up in a bit maybe, get something to eat with you; we'll see. But I gotta lay down now OK?"

Elsie supported Mary on her way to the bathroom. The sick woman pawed thru a collection of medications and finally asked the young girl to tear open an Alka Seltzer maximum strength package. Mary popped the tabs into a cup of water and downed the mixture. She let Elsie lead her back to the bed and tuck her in.

Nate stood at the open refrigerator door but couldn't decide on any of it's limited options. Lou popped open one cabinet after another, and finally spotted a packaged noodle mix.

Stroganoff, cup of water, cup of milk, dab of butter, microwave for 8 minutes. She directed Nate over to the dinette, where Elsie was seated. The truck stop phone lay on the table, screen open to a page for Spanish Fork.

Lou set about making the pasta, getting out plates and sodas, putzing about, making herself busy. Nate picked up the phone, scrolled thru it a bit, wondering where to start.

"Traci with an 'eye'? Last name of... ?"

"Carter, our name. Mom's name, her maiden name. Maybe that's Aunt Traci's too."

Hmmm.. He did a google search. Traci Carter- Utah and got a zillion hits.

Lou watched this exchange, thinking hard. Trying to remember something.

"Els, that first afternoon she was over, when she visited, she mentioned her job, it was different, I remember thinking it was cool, it was, it was.."

"Animals, cats! Er, dog, yeah, dog do's!"

Nate said "Dog do? Doggie doodoo? Cleaning dogshit out of yards?"

Elsie laughed. "No, hairdos ya dope. washing 'em, ah,

grooming! Yeah, she was a dog groomer!"

Nice! That gave them something to work with. He punched in 'pet grooming' and got a respectable number of results. 5 shops, one national chain, several individuals. No one using any version of Traci or Carter connected with a business. Nine numbers to call, messages to leave. Messages that say what?

The three of them discussed it while eating the pasta. How much detail to give, which of their phones to use, how to react if they reached a live person. The mood was upbeat even as the storm rocked their warm little refuge, snow swirling about.

The blinds were drawn tight, one of the things Mary showed them during their first night onboard. She explained she didn't want any 'peepers', which drew laughs from the kids. Now they liked the idea of privacy, just them inside. The lights were low, conserving the battery. Elsie had cleared the table, tossing the paper plates and plastic utensils. Dinner was over.

Nate had a paper and pencil, was doodling, thinking out loud.

"It has to be one of you, she's YOUR aunt. Just ah, say ah, say your name, say you're looking for your Aunt, your Mom's sister. Say your Mom's name. Ah, you met last year in Nebraska, and ah, I guess, call back. Right? Something like that?"

Both girls nodded. Else volunteered, took the paper, started writing. 'Hi I'm Elsie Carter, looking for my Mom's sister. Mom is Arliss Carter. We met you in Nebraska. Please call us Traci, number is 555 705 2142'

It looked like a lot to say, like a long message that no one would listen to. Especially coming from an unknown contact, a kid no less. But it was something specific, something written down. From starting with nothing, they'd come up with a script and were taking meaningful steps to locate Traci. They liked it, it was a good plan.

Lou had listed the names and numbers for the Spanish Fork groomer results. Elsie started to work thru the list, leaving a pretty good recording on a couple and taking time to critique it afterwards. She used the new truck stop phone to call but left Mary's number on the message. Mary's voice mail was setup.

Nate had an internal debate about contacting Sam. He really wanted to, it would be the right thing to do, he knew she'd be worried about him after days of not hearing anything. But he was still afraid to use his phone, didn't want to be tracked, wasn't ready to be located. So the question became, use Mary's phone or the new burner phone? Would a text be better? Yes, in the sense of the sister's not overhearing a call. He didn't know why but he felt a need to keep Sam and Elsie... separate. Right now anyway. So the boy sat quietly as the calls were placed over the next twenty minutes. Lou made the final two.

The blizzard kept up it's assault on their cozy little world, rocking them sternly at times, the sound of the snow peppering the exterior walls and windows rising and falling.

Nate nodded off towards the end. He turned in, cycling thru the bathroom then crawling into the overhead compartment. The girls could hear him snoring over the sound of the storm.

They setup the dinette as their sleeping platform and took their turns in the bathroom. Their last action before lights out was plugging both phones into chargers. The girls had high hopes for an incoming call.

CHAPTER TWENTY TWO

FIRST NEWS

Angela was a terrible driver in good weather, on flat open roads, mid-day, mid-summer. Rain, snow, wind, ICE or rumors of same terrified her. Her hand eye coordination degraded, her vision shrunk to a narrow cone, her ears thundered with tinnitus. Yet here she was, driving West on I 80 with the wind throwing hard pebbly sleet against her windshield. The storm warnings were legit, she wished she'd heeded them now.

She was at the wheel of a world class traveling machine, a one-year old Ford Explorer. A vehicle with the potential to go thru any terrain imaginable but at the timid and fearful hands of Angela, it wasn't even in four-wheel drive. As a result, her journey was an ordeal.

The retired woman had left Laramie hours before, heading home to Rock Springs. But now it was obvious she wasn't going to beat the storm, wasn't going to get home tonight. Instead, she was faced with this horrible situation on the road. Terrifying thoughts kept racing in, the wind would blow her off the highway, the snow would blind her, she'd crash and kill a poor, innocent baby. The building anxiety was becoming unmanageable, she had to stop.

And there it was, the sign for the rest area, 2 miles! Two miles, she could do that! The wind picked up, the snow fell more intensely, her speed dropped. The woman couldn't stay in her lane, her truck was all over the road yet she pushed on.

Finally, the exit to the rest area was at hand, the end of her perilous travel. There weren't clear tracks to follow as she edged over to the right to enter the oasis. Snow had drifted in spots. Her movements were jerky, she'd turn a little too sharply then overcorrect. The SUV faithfully responded to her inputs and careened back and forth as they left the interstate behind.

Angela spotted the rest area building. Parked cars were scattered along it covered in varying depths of snow. In front, just past the handicapped spaces, was an opening. The next space was occupied by a vehicle completely covered in snow, partially in her lane. So covered, it blended into the general whiteout Angela was struggling with. She did see it, eventually, but it was too late.

The Explorer clipped the left rear corner of the non-descript car; crushed it would be a more accurate description. Much to her dismay, air bags deployed, and she was smacked in the face. Her bad day just got worse.

Ten minutes later, a Wyoming state trooper was on the scene, processing a fender bender to end his shift. Well, the scheduled end of his shift; with the storm here now, it was all-hands on deck. He anticipated the highway closing in the next three or four hours, making this rest stop pretty important. Which made clearing this jacked up SUV a priority.

Officer Nemitz was standing at the driver's open window.

"Ma'am, I'm aware that you're upset but you have to listen to me. This vehicle is impeding traffic. Either you back it up and take a second attempt to pull up to the curb or get out and I'll do it myself."

She blubbered for a half second, then popped the door open and hopped out.

"Stand over there, in front of the car you hit. Yes, right there." He pointed. The officer slid behind the wheel of the idling Ford and pushed the airbag out of the way. Three seconds later, the truck was in place. He exited and guided the driver back to his cruiser which was then moved to a spot across from the damaged vehicles. Parking places remained available in the rest area but cars were steadily arriving. There were no departures.

A tow was needed for the Explorer but it had to wait for the storm to end. All available crews were working to keep the few lanes still open cleared.

The cop gathered her information and broke the news that she was basically stranded here. Well, not HERE, not in his cruiser but either in the Explorer or the heated, lighted, rest-room equipped building 60 yards away. Her choice. He would finish writing this report and then had to get back out on the road.

Angela processed her options and decided to stake a claim on a few square feet inside the building. She got out of the car and walked head down into the wind-driven snow, crossing over to her driver's door. What to take? Purse with phone, ah, bottle of water, whatever. She snatched just the purse, then slammed the door closed. A couple of others were hurrying into the rest area, getting ahead of her, damn! She locked the doors and scooted across the sidewalk, arm up to block the wind. The day couldn't get worse

She didn't notice Office Nemitz standing at the rear of the parked car she hit but he noticed her. She clutched her purse and hurried inside. She wasn't dressed for being out. But he was.

His state issued winter gear was flexible, layered. This

outing didn't need the full suit up with boots; it amounted to a quick survey of the parked vehicle's make and plates. He brushed off the license and read it, then took a swipe on the trunk to get the model. Cutlass. A cursory glance at the damage indicated the old GM was probably totaled. He walked around to the side and brushed off the windows there. His flashlight showed the front and back empty, nothing noteworthy visible on the seats or floor.

Satisfied, he returned to his warm car and punched the Nebraska plate into his laptop.

"My my, look what Interstate Eighty puked up for me tonight. A 2006 Dodge Intrepid. Isn't that curious. I coulda swore I saw a piece of junk Cutlass attached to that tag."

He flagged the entry and then exited his squad one more time, returning with the VIN off the car's dashboard. And a search of THAT proved it was flagged, surprise surprise. That VIN triggered alerts to flow, low level ones, small font and limited distribution but still alerts. Officer Nemitz grunted as he processed the missing vehicle/missing person notation. He'd have to go out one final time and sweep the building looking for the kid. If the boy wasn't there, he at least made the effort.

This was rinky-dink crap, a fender bender and a runaway.

Everybody inside was out of danger and safe. Folks still out on the road, not so much. He was needed out there.

He got out yet again and went into the rest area itself. A couple dozen people including Angela the ditz were in the lobby. He'd seen the runaway's picture, Nate, on the computer so the cop had a specific face he was looking for. An old man came up, asking about getting home. The room quieted, eyes turned towards the uniform, seeking guidance, reassurance and authority. It happened all the time.

"You're all safe here. You're warm, and dry so stay put, take care of each other. There'll be more arrivals as the storm gets worse, make room for them too."

His eyes swept the crowd of faces, no teen on the run. "Get comfortable folks, wait the storm out, few hours maybe overnight, we'll get things moving in the morning. OK?" He didn't wait for a response.

A quick walk thru the men's room, and a verbal confirmation of no males in the lady's room soon had the officer back outside. He made his way to his still idling unit.

The laptop screen had an update showing the Intrepid plate linked to a vehicle in a car lot in Ogallala Nebraska.

So the runaway from Minnesota has the presence of mind to snatch plates three hundred miles from here, and kept going. He'd pushed on, made it this much farther. But the kid was stopped now. Apparently stopped.

He estimated the car had been here the better part of the evening judging by the snow on it. Hours for sure. Breakdown? Arranged meeting? With any luck, the surveillance cams would show something. If they were in working order. He added a couple notes to his entry on the laptop and told dispatch he was headed back out.

Angus MacDonald awoke abruptly in his Vegas hotel mini-suite, in pain. His body ached, a low-grade headache made its presence known, and the dryness in his throat indicated snoring. Then his phone pinged, again. It was right next to his ear on the bedside table. The ping was for a new message.

He quickly threw aside the covers and sat up. 11 according to the LED alarm clock. He opened his phone and saw a text, from the Sheriff!

"Car found. Call us"

AT LAST!! He was euphoric, this was what he was waiting

for! As the news sank in and he re-read the message, his excitement dropped, a lot. Car found. Not Nate found.

He was flooded with emotion, relief, anxiety, fear, maybe some hope, yeah, gonna focus on hope. He held that thought as he dialed the office. It seemed to take forever to be answered, his sense of time was all funny.

"Olmsted County Sheriff's Department, my name is Deputy Gonzalez, how may I help you?"

"Hello, yes Ma'am, my name is Angus MacDonald. I filed a stolen car, missing person report with Olmsted County, on Saturday. I just got a message that the car has been located. It didn't say anything about my son, Nate, his name is Nate. Can you check for me please Ms Gonzalez?"

She confirmed the spelling on his name before placing him on hold. Another interminable wait. 'Please please, make him be OK' cycled thru his thoughts.

"Mr. MacDonald, this is Detective Spanner, I have the report in front of me. Your Cutlass has been located at the Fort Steele rest area. In Wyoming sir, a rest stop on Westbound Interstate 80. It was involved in an accident while parked there, apparently abandoned"

Blackie thought about that, Wyoming! He wished he had a map so he could see exactly where it was. The Detective continued.

"It was spotted around 8PM tonight. Your car had stolen plates Mr MacDonald. I don't suppose you know anything about that do you sir?"

Wait, WHAT?

"How in the WORLD would I know anything about that? Are you kidding me?"

"Nebraska plates, stolen from a car lot in Ogallala."

"No officer, I assure you, I don't know anything about that. What about Nate, he wasn't with the car, wasn't around it, hasn't shown up anywhere?"

"There's a storm sir, a blizzard. An officer walked thru the rest stop where the car was found but didn't see your son. It's a fluke, if the fender bender hadn't been blocking access in the rest area, the car wouldn't have been noticed for another day or more. The patrolman saw the missing person report and walked thru the building for a quick look, went a little above and beyond. It's possible your boy is still there, Mr MacDonald, we just don't know, the officer didn't see him."

Well, that was a bit of a letdown. It generated as many new questions as it resolved. Wyoming, wow, how did Nate manage to get that far all on his own? Blackie was impressed with his boy. Worried too. If he isn't in the car and maybe isn't in the rest area, where could he be?

He asked the officer for contact info for the local authorities; that he was currently in Las Vegas but would be leaving for Wyoming within minutes. The detective provided a phone number and advised Angus to check the weather reports and road conditions before his departure.

Blackie sat for a second, gathering his thoughts. He obviously had to go right now. Hit the road, get up there. Check out, load up the rental and scoot.

First, where the hell is the Fort Steele rest stop? He quickly mapped it out. Seven hundred freaking miles. Ten, eleven hours. Non-blizzard drive-time estimate most likely, so he jumped to a weather link. Radar showed the worst of it moving out of the area, moving pretty quickly. So things could be passable by sometime in mid-morning when I'll be getting there.

His stuff was packed in five minutes, he stepped off the elevator in the lobby five minutes after that. He dropped off the keycard and grabbed the receipt. On the way out, he stopped to pound down a cup of coffee from a kiosk right by the parking ramp door and finally left the Rio Suites casino. On the road, got a destination. Gonna get some answers.

The rental had plenty of gas, Angus didn't plan on stopping for a hundred miles at least. He got on Valley View going south, then took Flamingo Rd over to I 15 Northbound. There was a fair amount of traffic even at this time of night. The bright lights of the Strip merged into the bright lights of Downtown. They gave way to darker sections of urban life, then even that ended. Soon he had Vegas in the rear-view mirror. Blackie got settled in behind the wheel and made himself comfortable for the long drive ahead.

The caffeine kicked in. He found a XM Blues channel to serve as a quiet background for his trip. It was great to finally have REAL news on Nate. The FIRST news since, well, Thursday. Boy, that night seemed like an eternity ago. And a million miles away from Blackie's present location.

The question of finding just the car kept returning to his thoughts. If the car was intact and parked in a literal oasis during extreme weather, that was good, had to be good. So Nate was probably in the rest area. After all, it'd be crowded as hell with the storm. Nate would be on the lookout for uniformed officers driving state patrol cars, would not be so stupid to be caught.

But, if that's the case, then shit. He IS caught. Or trapped.

Wait a minute - Oh shit, don't I mean Yay? The mad dash is over? Well yay if that's how it ends, that he stays put. Stays right in that place for how many hours, another nine? And knowing the cops will be back, to get the Cutlass. And the crowd will go home. Then what's a runaway to do?

That's a depressing line of thought, c'mon. Buck up man, the car turned up in one piece. You'll be able to see it, go through it, feel – wait, yeah, go through it. And find or NOT find the handgun. Jeebus, I guess this means there'll be some CLOSURE on the weapon. IF it's there, which come to think of it, is unlikely.

But it would be very, and I repeat, very embarrassing if the cops found it. Maybe even more so if they found it in his presence. Hmmm. Which way was he more screwed?

Another depressing topic. Did he want the gun to be there or be missing? Missing like Nate.

Or, missing WITH Nate? Maybe that's the way to think about it, have a positive attitude. Like, it will be protection somehow. Not, somehow, turned against him. Shit, there I go again.

CHAPTER TWENTY THREE
THIS ISN'T A JOKE?

Angus focused his thoughts on driving for a couple miles, swept the dash, cycled thru the mirrors. The road conditions were excellent, the storm was hundreds of miles to his north-east and moving away. The temps were dropping as a north wind came in behind the low-pressure vortex. Fast moving scattered clouds blew from West to East unseen overhead, matching the cross breeze he had to correct for on the highway.

The Arizona border was just a few miles ahead. He'd slice across the top corner of it then enter Utah. St George was just a little further in, the first sizeable city. Angus figured that would be a good place for a pit stop. He'd gas up, hit the can, grab an energy drink and a donut, have a smoke then get back on the highway, keep burning up the miles.

Sonny Landreth and Joe Bonamassa played a tasteful selection of original blues as he drove on thru the night. It was hypnotic the way the music matched his mood and complimented driving on a superhighway. The first few hours flew by.

It was 2AM. His just completed gas stop gave him the opportunity to examine the best route to take and it wasn't thru

Salt Lake. He'd dash east at Provo, get off this interstate, blast past Park City, hook up with eastbound I 80.

Blackie took the 189 exit in Provo and drove north thru the town. He passed thru Brigham Young University neighborhoods and then went up into the canyon on the state highway for sixty miles. Plows were out and effective, the driving condition were good trailing behind the storm.

His route turned east as he left Utah behind, and cut across Wyoming towards the freshly discovered Cutlass. It wouldn't be long now, he felt strongly that things were coming to a climax, an ending, hopefully a happy one.

The roads gradually turned worse as the swirling, gusting winds moved the fresh snow. He was behind a pretty big storm and his speed and direction slowly overtook the center of the system. The plows kept the roads passable or technically, 'open' for those brave enough to venture out, like Angus MacDonald.

##

The phone didn't ring; the girls stupidly muted it. It did however light the screen; that's what eventually woke Elsie. Missed call and voicemail! An hour ago, at one!

"Hey! HEY!, we got a message, a callback!" She reached

over and gave her sister's leg a shake. "C'mon, wake UP, listen to it with me! Hey Nate!"

Lou quickly rubbed her eyes and sat up but all she got out of Nate overhead was a grunt.

"Huh? Really, we got a call? I didn't hear it ring."

Lou reached for the phone but Elsie pulled it back, held it against her chest.

"I think we should listen to it together, all of us, don't you?"

Lou sat quiet for a couple seconds. The blizzard was diminishing. It was still windy but the gusts felt weaker. Nate had resumed snoring, Mary chimed in with a brief coughing spell. Finally, she said "There's your answer Sis. Want me to holler at those two again or can we just play it already? I mean, they're out of it, let 'em sleep. It's maybe our Aunt, or maybe just a crank or a wrong number. Either way, we'll let 'em know. OK?"

Elsie was dying to listen, she really had her hopes up for good news. She handed the phone to Lou, who played the voicemail message:

"Um, I don't know why I'm calling back, this is so unlike me, but yeah, I DO have a sister and she does have girls and I was out to see them last summer, so maybe, well, I gotta take a chance here 'cause family and stuff, so yeah. Call me back, anytime. Please girls, just call me back. My name is Traci, with an 'eye'."

The girls were dumbfounded. Could it be? They listened to the message three more times, tears welling up in their eyes. It was unbelievable and they SO wanted, NEEDED to believe!

Elsie noted the time. 2:30AM. It would be rude to return the call now, in the middle of the night. Wouldn't it? She looked at Lou

"She said anytime, whadya think? Call her back now? I mean, it's HER Lou, I just know it! Don't ya think? Now?"

Lou didn't know. She was excited too, this is GREAT and all. But should they wait, should Nate and Mary be in on the conversation? She couldn't make that decision, she didn't know what to do.

Elsie was tired of waiting, figured calling now couldn't make things worse in any way, really. It couldn't hurt. So she put the phone on speaker and punched the call back button. They listened to the phone ring back in Spanish Fork UT.

After five rings, a sleepy voice answered.

"Hello?"

"Um, Hi!, my name is Elsie, Elsie Carter. I'm here with my sister Lou, er Louise. I'm sorry to call and wake you up but we just listened to.." She was interrupted.

"Oh MY GOD, Elsie! This isn't a joke? Louise too! Girls, I'm Traci! I saw you last summer, in Nebraska! That message you left scared me, I didn't know if it was real.. but it WAS real, Oh my GOD, I'm SO glad you called back, I wasn't sleeping anyway. Wow, so what's going on girls, you, your Mom, what?"

Elsie proceeded to outline Mom's medical issue, which troubled Aunt Traci, then detailed how they'd joined forces with both Nate and later, Mary. Lou jumped in several times, first to say hi, then to add her interpretation of events as told by the older sister.

The call was loud enough and lasted long enough to get Nate out of his alcove. He paused briefly, excited by the excellent news of reaching Aunt Traci, then plodded back to the bathroom. Refreshed, he joined the girls at the table. The highlights of their adventure had been told, Traci was zeroing in on the current situation.

"As soon as we're done here, I'll call the hospital, find out your Mom's condition. Second, I need you to stay put, wait right there for me. I need your exact location in where, Rawlins you said? I'm guessing that's about four or five hours away. If Mary gets any worse you'll need to call 911 you hear? You keep checking on her, you'll be able to tell. Otherwise, I'm coming. Don't move! You kids wait! Got that?"

"Hi Traci, um Aunt Traci I guess. I'm Nate. We're currently at a truck stop in Rawlins Wyoming."

"Hi Nate! How you doing? I sure appreciate you taking such good care of my nieces!"

"Thanks. Yeah, I'm doing OK, WE'RE doing OK I guess. If you're coming, that means I don't have to do any more driving and with this weather, I'm REAL OK with that!"

Traci brought up a map and scoped out the distance between them, saw the truck stops in Rawlins, both of them, one West and one South of town. A couple questions put them at the second one, Higley Blvd. She fine-tuned her ETA, knowing precisely where they were.

The kids were really excited about making contact with Aunt Traci based on the very limited info they had. Now with her hitting the road, coming to the rescue so to speak, they could relax a little, they just had to hang tight.

"Anything else you guys? Should I contact anyone else? Nate, your father maybe? Does Mary have anyone do you know?"

Nate thought about his Dad; he was conflicted. Was he ready to surface? The Cutlass would be a big fat arrow pointing to a location not TWENTY miles from here. Close to him, but not zeroed in. He could continue to stay missing. But what WAS his goal? He started out going to Vegas, to connect with Sam. Is that still his destination? Or was his destiny altered by the chance encounter with the sisters?

With another adult arriving and taking over the responsibility for Mary's well-being, was Utah now a destination or a way-point?

He finally decided he didn't know enough right then to change his original goal, he'd go with the flow, see what Aunt Traci's arrival brought. Thinking of Sam filled him with guilt. The least he could do is let her know he's OK, he made it as far as Wyoming, that a quick text now will be followed up with a call in a little bit. He didn't want the girls, well Elsie especially, to overhear a conversation with Sam.

"I'd rather wait a little while for my Dad Aunt Traci, if that's OK. I ah, I'm just not ready, it's kinda hard to explain but I'd rather not right now. As far as Mary, I don't remember her mentioning family or anything, the girls might know something more."

Elsie couldn't recall family being in any conversation with Mary. The husband now deceased, she'd mentioned no children.

"I suppose we could go through her phone contacts. That's kind of sneaky I think, like spying on her or something."

Elsie said that while speaking on that very same phone, unaware of the irony.

Traci said you guys figure out if they wanted her to contact anybody, but she was signing off, was hitting the road. "Call me, say in 2 or 3 hours. That'll put me half way there, will give us both something to look forward to. Or call if something comes up, OK? You guys gonna be ok there for another, 5 or 6 hours? That would be 9ish?? You just hunker down, stay put right?"

All three kids said "Yeah."

Tracie closed with a "OK. See ya soon, love ya!"

Relief washed over them. Mary's health taking a bad turn coupled with the insane weather had taken a toll on their morale.

The road had put a mental strain on them, the worry, the car troubles, the cops on the lookout for their previous wheels. Every high seemed to come with a setback. But now the cavalry was coming! They could go back to being teenagers, and a tweener. Their mood soared.

The storm was ending, the winds were dying down. Gusts strong enough to rock the RV became fewer, the background howl of the wind lessened. The sound of trucks, snowplows actually, were heard on the interstate, battling to open the road again, to get the traffic flowing.

Nate was beat, the twists and turns of the last few hours had wrung him out, emotionally and physically. The stress was now replaced with exhaustion. But he had one more thing to do before crawling into dreamland. He had to send a text to Sam, to let her know he was OK.

He looked at the phone on the table and plotted how to get his hands on it. He needed to squirrel it away for just a couple of minutes, so he could send a text to Sam in private. There'd have to be some kind of distraction to allow him to grab it and take it up to his loft, or maybe the bathroom.

As he pondered his options, sitting there around the

dinette with the girls, the phone rang. CRAP.

Elsie announced "Aunt Tracie again!" and took the call with an excited "Hi there!"

It was apparent to Nate that it was a report on the girl's mother's condition and that while it wasn't great news, it wasn't like, she was like DEAD or anything. Which was good, a relief for sure, for the whole crew, but as the conversation dragged on, he grew more impatient, more tired, more pessimistic about access to that phone.

Then it hit him, he didn't have Sam's number memorized. He couldn't use that stupid phone even if he could sneak it away somehow.

Her number's in his phone. He'd have to fire it up to get the number and if he had to do that, he may as well just send it too. It meant ending his silence, getting back on the grid. Did he want to do that, after being so disciplined up to now?

He owed her a message. It really boiled down to that. He was a jerk for leaving her hanging like this. Plus his situation will be changing in just a few hours, once Aunt Traci arrived.

Screw it. He'd send the message and grab some sleep, deal with the coming events after hitting the sack. He really was running on empty, completely drained.

Elsie was still chatting with her Aunt, who apparently was calling from the road; she'd already left home on her trek to Rawlins. Lou was listening in, whispering things to her sister occasionally, keeping involved in the conversation.

Nate put his finger up to his lips and then pointed up to the overhead bed. Elsie nodded and dropped her voice into a whisper, Lou gave him a wave.

He slowly rose and made his way over to the bunk. Climbing up, he crawled in and closed the curtain behind hism. His backpack was up front, by the pillow. He reached in and flinched as his fingers encountered the gun. Funny, he'd mostly forgotten about it. Deeper in the pack he found his phone. Nate pulled it out.

CRAP, it was dead! Duh, how many days? Maybe he just wasn't supposed to break his silence, maybe fate was sending a message.

He reached further in, looking for the charger cable. Not there. Why wouldn't he keep the phone with the charger, he thought back to Thursday night, packing the bag?

Oh yeah, side pocket. A thrill when his fingers closed on it, pulling it out and unwinding it. He'd wisely packed both the USB and the plug for an outlet, which the bunk so handily had. How much juice would a text take? Not much, if it was a short one. So the charge time, even being stone dead, shouldn't take long either. He plugged it in, got the charging confirmation. He didn't know if just the act of powering it up would make it connect to a tower, probably would. His location would be available now, if someone was looking for it. And he bet his Dad would be.

That thought was both comforting sorta, that dear old Dad would care that much (or be that pissed), and also frightening. This is a turning point, another one on the adventure. One of several so far, and they've all turned out OK. In fact, real OK.

So what to say? He watched the phone display showing the power on status The conversation between the girls and Auntie appeared to be winding down based on what he overheard. Like the storm outside.

He was thinking of what message to send. 'Hey Sam, no worries, I'm ok and still coming, talk soon'? Is he still coming, does he know that? Does he believe that? He had a throbbing headache and was super tired. The need to get this over and just lay down was overwhelming. Another minute and the phone was booted up, and now starting to charge.

'Hey Sam'... then what? Tell her a lot or a little? He opened the text window and typed in the 'Hey Sam' and hesitated, before finally entering 'I'm OK - in a Rawlins WY truck stop , car died, in a RV now, riding with some others. Will figure out what comes next, will let you know. Can't wait to C U'

He looked at it and then impulsively hit send. In a couple seconds he got the timestamp. 3AM. That was it then, officially. He'd surfaced. Things are in motion. Do I leave the phone on for her reply? What if she calls, that would be awkward. He wasn't sure exactly why but he didn't want to be overheard talking to Sam. By Elsie. His face got red just thinking about it.

He unplugged the phone and turned it off, deciding he'd continue to manage the incoming traffic by being deliberately offline.

But he also felt a whole lot better about letting Sam know what was going on, where he was and that he's OK, kinda saying he'd see her soon. Kinda.

The phone and cable were returned to his backpack. The vehicle was silent, the girls had conked out too.

His head hit the pillow and Nate was instantly asleep.

CHAPTER TWENTY FOUR
WIPE DOWN THE CAR

Maynard G was pissed. This weather was wearing on him, messing with his plans. Instead of prepping for Monday morning's meeting, the most important meeting of his life, he was stuck, literally stuck, in a goddamn snow drift in this podunk prairie town.

The stolen rental car was all wrong for a blizzard. He knew that now, when it was too late. Hell, he'd known it when Willie showed up with it yesterday afternoon in Denver. Of course, if they'd left on time, he woulda been here hours ago, ahead of the storm. But no, he had to deal with that dumbass brother of Fat Jake. Again. The fool had smacked some bimbo around in public. Caught on video. The cops were called, it was a big mess, a big time-sucking mess.

When Maynard was finally able to get the lawyers downtown, and get Fredo out of the can, it was midnight. He wisely hit the road without confronting Punchy McNum-Nuts; he couldn't risk ruffling any of Fat Jake's feathers before this meeting. This pow-wow will sanction Maynard G as the official voice of Fat Jake during the boss's unfortunate and lengthy incarceration. Maynard G will be the virtual Don.

Willie was Maynard's bodyguard/minion, currently stuffed behind the wheel of the pissant car that was 'borrowed' from the car lot across town. A lot that Fat Jake had a convenient interest in. It was a very small car for a very large man. TWO very large men.

Serves him right Maynard thought, as they drove into the worsening storm. At least Willie had the good sense to keep his mouth shut. Maynard hated a whiner. Especially when Maynard himself was all bent out of shape.

Since the little Nissan was worthless in the driving wind and the hard packed snowdrifts they encountered, Maynard G's attendance at the meeting was at risk. Willie's winter driving skills or lack thereof were also a factor in their current infuriating situation.

It was 6 AM and they were on the edge of a freeway off ramp, actually over the edge, on the prison exit. Willie had slowed to make the turn, but he got too far to the left and got sucked into deep snow along the shoulder. The vehicle had lost its forward momentum and finally came to a halt, totally hung up on a two-foot snowbank. Both doors were pinned by the snow and the front drive wheels were off the surface, the nose of the car riding up the drift

Maynard was cursing, pounding on the dash, demanding "Punch it ya dumb FUCK. C'mon, c'mon, don't stop goddamit!"

But it was too late. They had most definitely already stopped. Several minutes of Willie revving the engine, jamming the tranny back and forth in forward and reverse, imploring the Fates to get them unstuck only left them dug in tighter. Maynard raised his hand, signaling 'STOP'. The car idled, raggedly. The thirty year-old gangbanger sat there, his face bright red with fury, breathing hard. Finally, "Get out ya bum, get the fuck out and push. I'll drive!"

The storm was winding down, the snowfall had just about finished. The wind had dropped a bit but the new snow was still very much in motion. The temperature was 14 and dropping.

With the snow packed tight against both doors, it took quite an effort to get them open enough to squeeze out. Neither man was remotely dressed for the conditions. Without boots, their pant legs pushed up, with freezing snow pressing against their bare flesh, socks and flimsy shoes soaked.

Maynard G went to the front, a string of curses thrown

against the wind. He bent down to look under the nose of the car. Packed solid. The front tires, lifted off the road, had snow filling the wheelwells. He ineffectively kicked at the area in front of one tire, trying to open a space to allow forward movement. He struggled over to the drive's side, kicking the snow out of the way on that tire with his now numb and club-like right leg. He swung the door open and collapsed inside behind the wheel, slamming the door shut.

The snow on his clothes, especially his legs and feet, piled onto the floor as he brushed off. The heater was on full blast.

"Dammit, dammit DAMMIT!" He beat on the steering wheel and the dash in fury. He was freezing cold, soaked to the bone, shivering and enraged. Time to get this clown car going again, get them back on the road. Willie had fought his way to the rear. He punched the button to unroll his window, flinching as snow came cascading in, catching him right in the face.

Maynard shrieked towards the huddled figure leaning on the bumper "Are you ready GODDAMMIT??"

Willie's response was a miserable double thump on the trunk. Maynard G threw the tranny into drive and mashed the accelerator to the floor. Nothing happened. Well, the desired forward movement didn't happen, as the front tires remained suspended above solid pavement, spinning fervently inside the already frozen hollows molded earlier. Maynard screamed "PUSH PUSH, GODDAM YOU PUSH!!" and poor Willie, spent to the point of exhaustion, feebly went thru the motions at the rear, unable to affect the car's ice-locked status.

Without warning, Maynard jerked the tranny into reverse. The car's inertia subtly shifted from the front to the rear, but it remained trapped. The engine's noise rose as the rpms increased, the transmission contributing its own high-pitched whine. In a panic, Willie struggled to the side, unwilling to be a speedbump in Maynard's desperate escape attempt should the car achieve any traction. He finally leapt sideways into a drift to get out of the Nissan's potential path.

Unexpectedly, loud bangs accompanied by metallic grinding replaced the engine noise. A sudden belch of black smoke rolled out from the hood. A final tortured clatter was followed by silence. The ticks of overheated components expanding, a scorched, hot, burnt oil and electrical insulation smell enveloped the men.

"SEE WHAT YOU DID WILLIE, goddammit you BROKE the

FUCKING CAR! ARRRGGHHH!"

Maynard G sat for a moment then violently flung the door open and exited the still smoking wreckage. He stood shin deep in the snow and got his bearings. It was almost 7AM, not yet daylight. He had 3 hours until his appointment at the Wyoming State Penitentiary visitor center and he was NOT going to miss it, no sir. The wind and blowing snow were easing, he could see lights on the other side of the interstate. Not that far away, less than a half mile.

"Wipe down the car and grab our bags Willie. C'mon."

He strode off down the ramp, to the boulevard, to the lights, to warmth.

The drifts were tough to plunge through; his legs and feet had already lost feeling, making him unsteady. Between the bands of deep snow were stretches of bare pavement where progress was easier. Willie caught up with Maynard in 40 yards. The lackey looked beleaguered, physically as challenged as his boss but weighed down with two duffle bags and a large carryon. Much to the surprise of them both, Maynard grabbed a duffle and lightened Willie's load.

They crossed over the interstate as they headed south. As

the lights of the parking lot got closer, they were able to pick out details. One of which was a boxy, snow covered shape on the closest edge of the lot. With lights dimly visible, it looked warm and inviting.

# #

Blackie's Iphone lit up in the console, the blue tooth connection chirped the news of an incoming text on the dashboard screen and thru the sound system.

Nate's phone hit a tower!! The car, and now the phone!

Blackie couldn't believe it! At first, he stared at the message, reading it over and over. Nate! Back on the grid! He had to stop and process this, get more info, right NOW!

He tried to recall any upcoming places to stop, and yeah, Rock Springs was close, truck stop there, that'd work. A ton of different scenarios ran thru his head before he finally reached the turnoff, pulled into the truck stop and shut down his rental.

There was a contact number for his trace, he had it written down, but it also came with the text message. A long wait before his call was answered, but it was and by a real human to boot.

"Verizon Services, my name is Derrick, to whom do I have the pleasure of speaking?"

"Hey Derrick, my name is Angus. My son is missing, I just got the alert to call you, his phone has been used?"

Blackie gave adequate verification to appease Derrick and was told that Nate's phone contacted a tower in Rawlins WY at 3:05AM and sent a text message. The tower coordinates were 41.776 by -107.223. He wrote that down.

"Who was the text to?" he asked.

Derrick wouldn't say.

"What was the content of the text?"

Unsurprisingly, Derrick again demurred, repeated the agreement concerning the alert limited the company to providing the time, duration and location of the connection.

The call ended with 'thanks for the prompt response, it's enormously helpful, much appreciated, thank you thank you' and then Blackie took a minute to process what he'd just learned.

He quickly mapped Rawlins WY. A hundred miles! He was close to Nate, he just knew it! The map showed it was twenty some miles from the Fort Steele Rest stop to Rawlins. How did Nate get from the Cutlass to Rawlins? Or maybe, how did Nate's phone cover the distance?

He was standing outside, taking a smoke break and

stretching his legs. It didn't really matter he decided. Rawlins was closest, was the most recent clue. He'd already been told Nate wasn't with the car, apparently wasn't at the rest stop so it made sense to get to where the phone surfaced less than an hour earlier.

As he gathered himself to return to the road, Blackie paused. Text message, wouldn't it be great to learn to who and what it said? Obviously, it wasn't to ME, but it would very likely be to Sam. He decided to call her before taking off again. But she was pretty banged up, not conscious. Colleen got the call.

Her phone went to voicemail right away.

"Hey Colleen, this is Angus. Sure hope you're doing OK, Sam too! Say, I was just told Nate used his phone! Or, well, his phone was used, but it's gotta be him. Anyway, he sent a text. Did he send it to Sam? I'm hoping she's OK and maybe has her phone and you could check, see if she got a text from Nate? Please give me a call when you get this please, OK, um, yeah, prayers up for Sam, Colleen. I'm sure things will work out OK. Call me call me, thanks!"

#

Considering what they'd both gone thru, Sam's phone was

in significantly better shape than the girl herself. The teenager was of course, still hospitalized. She had recently regained consciousness, always a good sign, and was sitting up.

Colleen was overcome with relief, now that her baby woke up and was coherent. The mother had a black eye herself, getting worse as the hours went by. Along with a headache. The staff told her it was classic airbag-deployment symptoms. But she uttered no complaints about her own condition, her total concern was for Sam. And here she is, awake and talking, thank you Jesus!

Protocol required Sam to go thru a series of cognitive tests and Colleen sat next to her daughter while the doctor's quizzed her.

The testing paused for a few minutes, another part of the formal process, giving the subject a break to compose themselves if needed.

Sam had been talking things thru with her mom in the past half hour. Colleen filled in the timeline, updated her on what she knew about Angus' situation. Nothing from him, nothing from Nate...

"How would you know Mom, Nate would call ME. Where's my phone, where's yours?"

Colleen was a little taken aback. Their stupid cellphones weren't very important in the last few hours. But yeah, she didn't have her phone either! And yeah, that's a pretty good question, where ARE the phones? If they're lost, we gotta get replacements. Like soon!

Then the questions from the medical staff started up again. Colleen squeezed her daughter's hand and stepped out of the room. The nurse's station down on the left was pretty quiet at five AM. She asked the middle-aged RN what personal affects came in with her and Sam, if any. It just so happened that their purses, keyrings and PHONES all made it from the accident scene to a locked strongbox on their unit. They were lucky, that wasn't always the case.

CHAPTER TWENTY FIVE

B & E

Maynard G had come up thru the ranks, which meant starting out as a goon. Strong-arming people, sure. Hired muscle, throwing the fear of Mr. Big into somebody, all the time. And that included armed invasions. Bust down the goddam door, make a lot of noise, catch 'em in bed, that too.

Except this time was different. The goddam tiny goddam door knob on the goddam RV was impossible to grasp. His frozen fingers couldn't get a grip, the desired FLING of the door, banging it off the siding, didn't occur. His Grand Entrance was more of an Epic Fail, a scrabbling, slipping off the locked handle, dropping his gun in the snow while doing so, clown show. His racking cough contributed to the scene, alerting everybody inside to his presence.

Mary was already up, making coffee. The girls had fallen asleep a couple hours earlier, Nate a half hour after them. The old woman was feeling somewhat better after some decent sleep and her meds. She was just about to peer out the windshield, to check the weather, when she heard something outside. A noise, voices? Some coughing, yes, two men she realized, two men coming closer.

She froze in place, empty coffee pot in hand, staring at the door. Lou heard it too and sat up, rubbing her eyes. Nate's head appeared out of the overhead bunk, taking in the scene. They were all moving past surprise and shock, getting into the terrified stage. And then sounds that could only be attempts to get inside!

The door! They were trying to open the door, trying to break in! Loud hammering rattled the glass, the handle itself shook, the flimsy lock was sure to let go any second. Elsie couldn't help herself, she let loose with a piercing scream. That was followed by a harsh reply from the outside.

"Open this goddamn door girlie!!"

Elsie stuffed a fist in her mouth but too late, girlie had outed them. Not that it mattered. The thugs were determined to get in.

The kids looked towards Mary for adult reassurance but alas, Mary wasn't up to the task. The intruder's shout shattered her fragile recovery. The coffee pot fell to the floor sending glass everywhere. Mary also dropped, also to the floor, slumping down gracefully in slow motion.

The pounding, knocking, and banging on the door

continued.

"Goddammit I AINT KIDDING GODDAMMIT! Open this door NOW!"

Elsie slipped out of the dinette/bed and ran carefully over to Mary, sobbing over the unconscious woman. Nate felt obligated to speak, buy them a couple moments.

"COMING, COMING man, don't break the dam door!"

Nate dropped to the floor and looked very pointedly at Lou. She was white faced, trembling, but still hanging in there. She looked intently back at the boy.

He made the universal sign. A closed fist, index finger out, thumb up. He shook it, twice, then motioned up, to the overhead bunk. He mouthed 'BACK PACK' and waited for acknowledgement.

A pause, then her eyes narrowed, and she nodded. Twice.

Nate gave her a thumbs up and a smile, then yelled out "Coming, coming!" as he crossed the RV and opened the door.

The two thugs didn't enter the RV as much as collapse into it. Nate stood back as they untangled themselves and struggled to stand. Willie sliced his palm open on glass from the coffee pot when he pushed himself up, adding to his woes. When they were finally all the way in, the boy closed the door, locking the six of them in together.

A pregnant pause as the men stomped their feet and beat their arms against their chests. Their breathing was very ragged as they stood there in frozen, wet clothing. Maynard noticed the blood pouring out of Willie and let out a fresh string of curses, finally pointing at Lou and barking "You! Stop his bleeding now!"

She scrambled to the bathroom for a towel.

"Turn the heat up, ALL THE WAY UP, right NOW!" he yelled, glaring at Nate. The boy didn't know, exactly, how to change the thermostat. It was Mary's RV, it was just set somewhere. He nervously started looking around. Elsie looked up from the floor, where she was cradling Mary's head. She remembered Mary fiddling with it.

"In the cabinet, over the door."

She pointed to the entrance so recently breached. Sure enough, there was a panel that controlled the heat and AC. Nate punched a couple buttons, figured out which did what, and soon very hot air was pouring done on the occupants.

Lou returned with a thin wet towel. She wanted to hand it to Willie and retreat, but he grunted and stuck his hand out instead. She dabbed at the bloody palm ineffectively and finally wrapped it loosely and tied it off. The towel started to turn red.

Maynard noticed the old woman and the girl on the floor.

"What the hell is wrong with HER? and you, YOU get up!"

With silent tears streaming down her face, Elsie shook her head and refused to leave Mary's side. She stuck out her chin and said "Her name is Mary, this is HER home. She's sick, can't you see that?" The girl bent down over her friend, not budging.

Her sharp response caught him off guard. He decided they could stay put, waved his hand to indicate that. He had other priorities right now. Number one was getting OUT of these wet cold clothes. He scoped out the interior and walked back to peek in the bathroom and bedroom.

"Keep the kids covered, keep them QUIET! I'm gonna dry off and change for my meeting. Your turn when I'm done."

He glared at the kids, then spoke again.

"Show 'em Willie."

His blood-soaked left hand pulled back the unlined leather jacket, exposing a holstered handgun.

"You go ahead and shoot 'em if they make a sound, got that?"

Willie nodded and looked at each kid in turn.

Maynard issued directions to move Mary to the dinette/bed and to get that broken glass picked up. A quick whisper into his henchman's ear and then the boss took his duffle bag into the bedroom, shutting the door behind him.

Willie spun the passenger seat around and sat down. He waved for the kids to get going. Elsie and Lou bent down to pickup the larger pieces of glass off the vinyl floor, dumping them into the waste basket. Nate arranged the dinette and then joined the sisters in coaxing Mary back to consciousness.

A wet paper towel on her forehead was rewarded with eyes that fluttered open. Soothing words and a couple of arms soon got her upright. After resting a minute, she was assisted in a shuffle over to the girl's bed. A brief coughing spell was forthcoming, then she zoned out again. Elsie felt her forehead; even after the wet cloth, she was able to detect a fever.

"This woman is SICK! She needs to see a DOCTOR! Now!"

Willie brought his forefinger up to his lips and shook his head.

"The boss said quiet, so shuddup, don't make him mad. You won't like him when he's mad."

This was followed by a menacing grin. Willie was shaking off the cold, was feeling a little more optimistic about pulling off this important meeting. His wagon was hitched to Maynard's, and their outlook had markedly improved over the last hour. He wasn't exactly clear on what the boss had in mind, what this new plan was gonna be but they were inside again and had wheels. He looked around the RV and pondered if the other occupants were their hosts or their hostages. Not that it mattered, it wasn't up to him, the boss would decide. Willie would just do what he's told, like always.

Maynard G's movements in the bedroom could be felt in the rest of the vehicle as the large man moved about. He'd grabbed a towel out of the bathroom on his way back and once in the bedroom, peeled off his wet, cold clothes. He vigorously dried off under the very hot air blasting from the ceiling vent. The blower poured waves of beautiful propane-generated heat over his abused body.

Soon, he had clambered into clean, dry clothes. A dark turtleneck, sport coat and fitted jeans look that all the fashionably dressed mobsters were currently wearing.

As he transfered his wallet, money clip and phone into the

jacket, he started cursing; Cell phones! These civilians out there, those sneaky bastards, they might be dialing 911 on their goddam cell phones at this very minute. Those pricks!

Maynard burst thru the bedroom door, raising hell.

"Gimmie your goddam cell phones NOW goddammit! All of 'em!"

And impossibly, at that instant, the burner cellphone bought at the truck stop started ringing. There on the counter, display lit up, announcing an inbound call. Aunt Traci, getting close, checking in.

Lou instinctively jumped for it, scooting forward.

Willie's quick reflexes also kicked in, positive of Maynard's approval. He leaned over and slapped the girl, hard, on the side of the head. Boom - she dropped like a rock. Lights. Out.

Two more unanswered rings and the device went silent, directing the caller to voice mail. Everyone in the motorhome started talking/yelling/crying at once, breaking the shocked silence. Except for Mary. And Lou. Those two were oblivious to the commotion around them, they remained silent and calm.

CHAPTER TWENTY SIX
CONTACT!

Sam snatched the phone out of Colleen's hand, the mother a little peeved.

"Hey! I was giving it to ya!"

The girl let out a squeal. "A Text from NATE! I knew it! A couple hours ago .. it says…"

"Geez Mom, he's in, in Wyoming? He's OK! - in some truck stop parking lot! And car trouble? 'in a RV now, riding with some others' Huh? 'Will figure out what comes next, will let you know. Can't wait to C ya'. What the hell does THAT even mean?"

Colleen certainly didn't know. She wondered who the others could be, what kind of situation the boy found himself in. "Read it again honey."

Hearing the text a second time didn't clarify much but they both agreed it had a positive tone. Which was encouraging.

Sam started typing in a reply, asking Nate to call her, let her know what's going on, she was worried, had news of her own. She hit the send button and waited, waited. After 4 minutes, she got a delivery failed status. He had gone silent again. Mysteriously, frustratingly so.

Colleen started to talk about possible scenarios that might explain the cryptic message but stopped when the creepy, alarming explanations came to mind. There weren't a lot of happy, positive ways to interpret his text. They needed more info, an update, a live conversation.

The girl was bummed that her reply didn't go through. She was getting more worried about her friend after this update. Concerned about who he was with now and wondering what had happened on the highway. She was also feeling a little light headed again, her vision wasn't right. She needed to rest. Just a little nap, that's all, then she'd wake up and Nate would call.

"Mom, I gotta close my eyes, that light hurts 'em. You'll be here when I wake up won't ya?"

Colleen sprang to her side, patted her hand.

"You go on honey, rest up. Of course I'll be here. I won't move. You close your eyes, don't worry about nothing."

Sam nodded off within moments. Colleen had her daughter's phone, reading and re-reading the boy's text. She was tired too, it'd been a long day, including meeting Angus. Angus! She snapped alert. He needed to know this! She knew he'd left town, assumed he was backtracking East.

In the excitement of handing over her daughter's phone, Sam hadn't checked her own. Now, when she did, she saw a recent voicemail, from Angus!

She listened to the recording, knowing that yes, Sam did get the text, yes she had regained consciousness, yes things were looking up.

She called back. Angus answered on the second ring.

"Colleen! Thank God you called back. How is Sam, is she OK? And how are YOU?"

"Yes Angus, she woke up, she's gonna be fine. Broken arm, we both have black eyes, not a good look but we're real lucky. How are you, WHERE are you?"

"I feel like I survived a real live car crash and have the aches and pains to prove it but yeah, I feel super fortunate too. I'm on the road, in Wyoming. It's crazy, his car was found! I got contacted just a little bit ago! Found in a rest area, a couple hours away. Abandoned! I was headed there when I just got another alert, that Nate used his phone! In Rawlins Wyoming, sent a text. Did you get my message, did Sam get a text?"

"OH MY GOD, YES – We just got our phones, the hospital had them, locked up, purses too and... well I'm rambling but YES.

He said, um, he's in Wyoming, Rawlins, in a truck stop, yup, in a RV too. Had car trouble, like you said, abandoned, broken. Um was with some others, that's what he said. I wonder what that means ya know? But, he sounded upbeat, looking forward to seeing Sam, would let her know what's going on… Sam replied but her text wasn't delivered. But yeah, that lines up with the car being found, so if he's with someone, and they're in the parking lot, A truck stop, that's GREAT! Right Angus? Here, here's the exact wording…" She read the text to him, twice.

Wow. He was stunned. WITH somebody, what the hell does THAT mean? Yeah, it WAS great news, once he processed things for a second. The fact that the car was found without the boy was unsettling, and now to know that there was a semblance of an explanation for it, breakdown, caught a ride. So yeah, with somebody. In a RV no less. The troubling part is the nature of who he's with. He did take comfort in Colleens intuition about Nate's state of mind based on the text.

"Yeah, wow, thanks SO much Colleen! A RV huh? a truck stop, yeah that will let me zero right in on 'em, knowing that. And it's so great that Nate popped his head up. Yeah, it's fantastic that he contacted Sam, and that he's OK. And it looks like this whole adventure is going to wrap up smoothly, the way things are coming together fast now. I'm, ah.. fifty miles or so from Rawlins. Trailing the blizzard and the roads are you know, winter driving and all but they're plowed. Like back home."

"That's so exciting Angus, that'd mean an hour or so, right? You drive safe and get your boy. Then you CALL US, first thing, OK? We'll be, well I'll be up, Sam took a pain pill and is getting some rest right now, for a while I'm sure, but I'll be here, you CALL ME OK?"

After reassuring Colleen that yes, she'll be kept in the loop, first thing, sure thing, you betcha, he hung up. And Blackie's mind went into overdrive. Different pieces of the puzzle came into focus, then faded away. It was replaced by a different, unknown random factoid. RV. Traveling with 'others'. Car trouble. Truck stop. Blizzard. Oh and of course, the freaking gun, the cherry on top.

Damn son! What kind of drama have you got yourself into? He reflected for a minute, then laughed. You AND me, holy shit. Car crash, drug dealer, death! I guess drama runs in the family this crazy-ass weekend. Both of us, for sure. And we'll meet again, in a matter of hours. You're just down the road so hang on son, I'm almost there. Daddy's comin!

#

That was odd. They didn't answer. Traci quickly left a throw-away 'Aunt Traci, call me girls!' message and figured she'd try again in a bit.

She was excited that she'd be with the girls shortly, and they'd be safe again. Her sister did her best, but her addictions were powerful. For the most part she'd kept jobs, made a home for her daughters, taken pretty good care of them until about a year ago. Which prompted Traci's visit. Ever since, she'd had an feeling that this day might come, when Arliss hit bottom and the cavalry was needed. She never imagined these circumstances however, being called by the girls!

Traci gave thanks that her nieces turned out so well, based on her visit out there last year and on today's calls; the girls were sharp. Except they didn't pick up this last one. Maybe they'll call right back. Any minute now, any minute.

She was about an hour away, just east of Table Rock. The road conditions allowed a top speed of 60 or so, or a safe top speed in her opinion. The right lane was pretty clean, only snow covered in spots. The left lane wasn't as clear, making passing a slower vehicle a challenge. Traffic was very light, she moved along patiently and steadily closed the distance.

She was a little apprehensive about what exactly awaited her in Rawlins, in the RV. The elderly owner of which was ill, how ill she had no idea, nor what the illness was. What if it was something contagious!

And what about Nate? He seemed nice enough, for the little she'd spoke with him. The girls seemed to like him and that meant a lot. But it boiled down to him being a runaway, and in possession of, or formerly in possession of a car that was stolen.

She alternated between worrying about the unknown negatives and being grateful and relieved. She focused on getting into a positive frame of mind and put herself there. That mood would last for a few miles before another random crazy thought, like what if the cops got involved somehow, the truck stop called them, THEN what? Well, cops, that wouldn't be terrible, as long as it was something stupid like being in a no-parking zone or something. Then she'd question whether she wanted to deal with this herself, outside of law enforcement, or would welcome their involvement. Couldn't really tell what to hope for.

She'd know soon enough. 30 miles, half an hour. Hour

tops to get things straightened out. Which was comforting, coming up to the end of this escapade, a happy, peaceful ending for sure.

##

"QUIET!! Or do YOU wanna get smacked TOO?"

Elsie was at her sister's side, tears pouring out as she hugged Lou and wailed loudly. Nate clamped his mouth closed, in mid outburst. He was shocked, Willie's huge fist flicked out so darn FAST and unexpectedly! Hitting a girl like that! slapping her, that was really hardcore. The violence, dealt so casually, scared him a lot.

"Gimme your phones, NOW, all of 'em, right now, move it!"

He pointed to the now silenced one on the counter

"All of 'em, now, RIGHT HERE"

Nate and Elsie were the extent of the audience for these demands, with Lou and Mary being in LaLa-land.

Nate got up and gingerly handed that one to Maynard. The boy pointed to the overhead sleeping area, and moved across the motorhome, hoping and praying that the maniac wouldn't insist on retrieving it himself, or sending the other goon to do it.

Willie was dealing with the second phone that Elsie volunteered, pointing to its location.

Nate reached up and slipped his hands into the backpack. For a brief instant, he touched the weapon. A millisecond of hesitation before he sensed movement behind him. He spun around, cell phone in hand, offering it to a menacing Willie. The boy quickly moved away.

He looked at the three phones gathered on the counter. How stupid were they, watching the slow-motion invasion of their shelter, mouths hanging open, and they did NOTHING! These low-lifes come busting down their door, and with THREE easily accessible phones, did any of us dial 911? Oh hell no.

He dragged his eyes away and looked at the sisters. Too late for second guessing, he needed to think of what's next, how to react, how to protect the girls. He felt guilty that he'd already failed Lou, the littlest. But sadly it looked like he'd be at the mercy of their captors, they'd be calling the tune and he'd be the dancer. And just then, the song changed.

Maynard, yelling again.

"C'mon, get the kid and the old lady outa here."

Elsie's heart skipped a beat, she blurted out "NO!",

thinking he meant to toss them outside! Willie stepped up and gestured for her to help roust Mary, get her on her feet. He went back and opened the bedroom door and returned, looking expectantly at Elsie. She gently set her sister's head down and moved over to Mary.

"Mary, c'mon Mary, we're going back to bed, your bed, you can rest back there OK? Just sit up here, we'll help you get back there, that's it, a little bit more, here we go, you're doing great!"

The woman managed to get to her feet and shuffle back to the bedroom, propped between the girl and gangster. A coughing spell occurred but was brief. Mary looked at Elsie and said "I think I'm getting better, a little" but her eyes were messed up, rolling around in her head. The girl just nodded in agreement.

They laid her flat. Elsie covered her with an afghan, and Willie closed the door behind them as they left. He motioned Elsie over to Lou next and asked, "Where's she going Boss?"

He replied with a grunt and a head movement, indicating Nate's quarters above the cab. Maynard was now sitting up front, with Nate.

Willie grabbed the young girl under her shoulders, from

behind, and started dragging her over to the bunk. Elsie quickly picked up her sister's ankles and helped. As the goon hesitated to free up a hand to open the curtain, he turned his head. Elsie saw Lou's left eye pop open and focus on her. A quick smile followed by a definite wink surprised Elsie to the point where she dropped her sister's feet, -clump-, to the floor, prompting Willie to grunt and look back.

Elsie quickly wiped the shocked look off her face, and somehow managed to keep from smiling herself, as she bent down to refasten her grip.

A scowling Willie lifted Lou high and tossed her into the bunk, effortlessly, like a sack of potatoes. Elsie yelped and moved to check on the girl but was blocked by a big fist grabbing her shoulder, shoving her back to the dinette.

Maynard G was quizzing the boy on the operation of the rig.

Nate explained the controls and the gauges, then showed how the curtains rolled aside. Apparently, they were preparing to leave the truck stop. Elsie realized that could only mean one thing; they're being kidnapped! A million movie and television shows sprang to mind. The girl distilled them all to one horrifying essence; the outcome for the victims was usually bad!

She panicked.

"Party time Willie, time to get this goddam bus moving, what ya think huh?"

Willie checked his watch, saw they were closing in on the time for the big meeting, the whole point of all of this bullshit.

"Yeah boss, its time."

Maynard G started the engine, gunned it, then let it drop to an idle. He calmly said "Someone has to go outside, clear the wheels, scrape the windows front and back, and brush snow off the lights and mirrors."

Willie, who was still in his wet clothes from their earlier exposure, knew who that someone was. He got up and walked towards the door. The boss promised he could dry off and change when he was done out there. "Yeah boss."

He was thorough and efficient. Lights were brushed off as he checked the wheel wells; the driver's side needed a couple leg sweeps in front of the tires to clear them, the windshield and side windows were melting from the inside heater doing its job.

He stopped and took in the activity spread out to their left, with big rigs moving in and out, snow removal equipment finishing after the storm, the diner across the way filling up at breakfast time. The eastern sky was just beginning to lighten with the arrival of the new day. Willie went back inside, where he moved directly to the bathroom to dry off and change.

Nate got up the courage to start to ask a question, made it as far as "What are you.." when Maynard spun around and snarled "Shut up!" The boy decided not to provoke Maynard further and resigned himself to not having a scrap of info to go on. He'll have to go with the flow. With luck, some kind of opportunity would arise, with more luck, he'll be quick enough to recognize it and act. Certainly, he'll get SOME kind of chance!

After a couple minutes, Willie returned up front. He seemed in a better mood, brought about by the warm, dry clothing no doubt. Without comment, he joined Elsie at the dinette and faced the rear, sitting where he could view the outside door and the bedroom/bathroom. She noticed he'd redid the bandaged hand.

"I don't want any funny business from those two kids, this is serious shit. No trouble, am I clear?"

"No trouble boss." Willie responded.

The driver got situated; lights, seat, mirrors all adjusted

perfectly then he shifted into drive. The motorhome rocked a bit as it eased forward. Nate had pulled onto the north edge of the truck stop and shut down. To get onto the road, Maynard had to turn around. He ill-advisedly and impatiently started a sharp left turn without checking his surroundings.

A piercing airhorn blast startled him! An inbound cattle truck was right at his door, right in the path of his turn! He stood on the brakes, abruptly throwing his passengers forward. Quick reactions from both drivers kept the vehicles from colliding. The trucker flipped Maynard off as he barreled by, flaring his hair trigger temper briefly.

"WATCH WHERE YOU"RE GOING ya STUPID FUCK!"

The gangster sat for a moment, gathering his composure, lowering his blood pressure. It wouldn't do to be this close to the prize and carelessly piss it away. He had to get his shit together, start checking his mirrors at a minimum.

After painstakingly looking for any other traffic, he got them moving again. They made their way out of the truck stop and turned right, south, on Higley Boulevard. Wyoming State Penitentiary, two miles ahead.

CHAPTER TWENTY SEVEN
WHAT ARE THE ODDS?

The Flying J truck stop was a couple miles West of Rawlins. Blackie was pretty sure the alert his boy's phone triggered was right IN Rawlins, but hey, here's a truck stop, he had to be sure. So he pulled off the interstate to double check. He'd make it a smoke stop, stretch his legs.

The internet map showed this one and another right on the town outskirts. He double checked the tower coordinates he'd written down and confirmed it was the other truck stop. He was close, two miles, and couldn't wait to blast back onto the highway, get to the right spot. It was a minor delay, didn't add but maybe 10 minutes to his eventual arrival at the Rawlins Travel Center/Conoco truck stop, where Nate's phone surfaced. Maybe 15 minutes, tops. Trivial really.

# #

Traci noticed the flashing lights as she took the Rawlins exit. Across the overpass on her left, a tow truck wrangled a stranded vehicle. The truck stop passed on her right as she left the interstate; a quick scan didn't reveal an RV. A turn onto S Higley Blvd and then another right brought her into the sprawling complex. She decided to roll thru the entire lot in search for the girls.

Her slow, thorough tour thru the well plowed expanse didn't reveal any motorhome. She checked the adjacent properties, a hotel and truck service/parking area. Those lots were all full but also failed to yield the hoped-for RV containing the girls and their traveling companions. Traci got an uneasy feeling and took another loop, in the opposite direction. Still nothing. As she finally pulled up to the main building, a Nevada rental that was also doing a slow crawl around the lot crossed her path. She didn't notice, just stopped to let it go by as she angled into a parking place.

Traci took in the brightly lit layout as she stepped thru the doors. A Subway on the left, merchandise straight ahead. Down past the coolers and chips were the restrooms. The cashier area was on her immediate left, where customers funneled through to pay. Beyond those checkouts stood a long service counter.

A large variety of activations, money xfers, showers and bunks, scales, truck washes and everything else a commercial driver needed were handled there. She made a beeline to it and was greeted cheerily by Sally, according to her travel center badge.

"Good morning, welcome to Rawlins. My name is Sally. What can we do for you today?"

Traci didn't know how to start, and said so.

"Um, yeah this is gonna sound funny, I'm not really sure how to ask, er explain, well yeah, ASK is right, I'm looking for something that was in your parking lot before but now isn't?"

She screwed up her face in a grimace, expecting Sally to think she was nuts.

Apparently, that wasn't the oddest thing to be expressed at a truck stop service counter because Sally didn't miss a beat.

"Well honey, let's start at the beginning. My name is Sally, you are?"

"Yes, I'm sorry, hey Sally, I'm Traci. With an 'eye'."

"Hey Traci with an 'eye', I'll be happy to help you find whatever it is you lost."

A nervous chuckle. "No, I didn't lose.. it's not like that. It's just that my nieces were in the parking lot earlier, I talked with them, and they were in a RV, they said, some kind of motor home. Parked in your parking lot. I spoke with them ah, a couple hours ago. And I looked just now, I drove around and around your lot outside. And there isn't a motor home. And now I'm kinda worried, ya know?" She paused, looking, HOPING for some sort of acknowledgement that Sally could help.

"Oh honey, of course you're worried, ya got me worried now too! Let's get some details and we'll get looking for those girls!"

Sally waved her around the counter and spoke a few words to a coworker before taking Traci into an interior hallway. Once inside a small office, Sally said,

"Traci, just a formality, but can I see some ID please?"

She reached into her jacket and swiftly produced her license. Sally swiped it thru a reader next to a laptop on the desk, then peered at the monitor. She returned it with a smile.

"I'll be glad to help Traci. From sound of it, I think our surveillance recordings will do a pretty good job showing what went on out there the last few hours. But first, please tell me the story. Start at the beginning. Tell me about the girls, your nieces did you say? How'd they end up in our parking lot?"

Traci started way back, with the visit to her sister last year, "the first real time I met the girls, oh Elsie um 16, and Lou she's 11, my sister, has some issues with, well drugs and alcohol, and she's really tried hard to be a good Mom and the girls are just, super! Elsie really looks after her little sister and they're both really smart…"

"I stayed with them for a weekend, borrowed my sister some money. That was last summer. But I made a point to tell Elsie where I live and that, you know, look me up. I can help, we're family."

Sally, caught up in the story, nodded encouragement when Traci paused.

"OK, that was last summer. What's going on now?"

"Friday, my sister had a reaction, I guess you'd say she OD'd. The girls came home from school, saw their Mom being carted off. Child services tried to scoop them up. They ran instead. Somehow, and this part isn't real clear, they met a boy, another runaway. He was on his way to Vegas. And they joined up. Then their car broke down. Then they met up with some senior citizen named, um, Mary. She owns the RV. The three kids joined up with Mary. But she's pretty sick. So the boy, Nate, he was driving and then the blizzard hit and they pulled in here, last night."

She continued.

"Oh and I forgot, the girls remembered me! They remembered that I'm a dog groomer in Spanish Fork and the kids were resourceful enough to do a search, left a bunch of messages and one of them got to me! And I called back and we talked and talked and then I jumped in my truck and came straight here. To get Elsie and Lou. But they aren't here and now I'm worried and I don't know what to do..." She couldn't help the flood of tears that followed.

#

Angus made two loops, slow ones. The sprawling truck stop covered 15 acres total. The primary building oversaw the outlying gas and diesel islands, with various parking lots for both trucks and cars. No motor homes visible. A two-story motel stood behind the truck stop. A drive thru their lot revealed no RV.

He made his way back to the truck stop and parked in front of it's main doors. A quick check of his watch; 8:55. The last contact, supposedly from here, was about six hours ago.

If that were the case, then Nate was here, about twenty miles from the abandoned Cutlass. He WAS in a motorhome of some type, with some mysterious 'others'. With the current absence of any such RV, then obviously it left in the last six hours.

It wasn't particularly insightful to realize the truck stop was under thorough, constant video surveillance and would have recordings.

Inside, the checkouts were on his left, with a service counter beyond them. He headed there and waited briefly while a trucker sporting a black cowboy hat finished gathering his documents. The conversation he'd overhead revealed them to be faxed permits for hazardous materials, one of the truck stop's most valued services.

He noticed the employee's name from her badge. "Hey Lynne. My name is Angus, and I guess I have a favor to ask."

Lynne's eyes twinkled a little, hoping this one would be something new. She heard and saw a LOT on this job because the traveling public were incessantly entertaining. She could write a book!

"Well Angus, we aim to please here at the Rawlins Travel Center, so go ahead, tell me the nature of this favor and we'll do our best!"

"I'm hoping to review your video recordings, of the parking lot, the outside area. Going back like seven or eight hours maybe?"

He noticed Lynne's mouth drop open slightly, a very

puzzled expression on her face. He continued.

"It's kind of a long story, involving my son. He's a runaway and it ah, it appears that he was here. Not too long ago. In some kind of motor home, and..."

Lynne grabbed his arm across the counter, interrupting his explanation mid-stream. "Motor home? Really! you're looking for video of a MOTOR HOME in our lot TOO?"

It was Blackie's turn to be puzzled. He looked around, no one else was in line at the counter. His elbow was still locked in Lynne's grasp. She quickly let go but then he grabbed her hand.

"Whadya mean, too?"

"Not less than 10 minutes ago, someone walked in here, a woman, and asked the same thing, to check out our video. Looking for a motor home! What are the odds of THAT?"

Blackie's turn to be gob-smacked. Huh? Someone ELSE looking for a motor home? A woman, who the hell could THAT be?

"C'mon, follow me. She's in the back with my supervisor. I can't WAIT to introduce you!"

He walked around the counter and trailed behind Lynne as she navigated a series of hallways. She finally stopped at a door labeled Operations Center. Lynne knocked and then opened it. As they stepped thru, they heard two women in conversation.

"This is where our video feeds come in. It's monitored by these live security personnel and it's also recorded. What time did you speak with the girls, was it before the storm?"

Girls? Who were the girls? Angus cleared his throat, catching the attention of Traci and Sally.

Lynne said "Sally, please excuse us for interrupting, this is Angus. He just stepped up and asked for a favor. Angus, this is my boss, Sally. Please tell her what you need."

He stretched out a hand to Lynne's supervisor with a "Pleased to meet 'cha" and turned to Traci, did the same. He saw an attractive woman with red eyes and a concerned expression.

"Angus MacDonald, nice to meet you. And forgive me but you are?..."

"You're the boys DAD, of course!" She broke into a broad smile and grabbed his proffered hand, shaking it eagerly. Blackie responded with a puzzled grin, and nodded, 'Yup, that's me. The boy's, er Nate's father. And you are.."

"Traci! Angus, it's SO nice to meet you. My nieces, Elsie and Lou, they're with Nate! He picked them up in Nebraska. I spoke with all three of them, like four hours ago!"

Traci turned towards Sally, explaining for her, and for everyone really, the background. Stolen car, run-aways picked up, engine trouble, motorhome with some kind of guardian angel and finally ending up here, at the travel center.

Blackie soaked up this new information, puzzle pieces falling into place clink clink clink. A bigger picture. Nate took a couple sisters under his wing, how about that! The car being broke down in the rest stop and Nate arriving here in the motorhome cleared up a lot of confusion. But it didn't answer the question of where they were right now.

He asked "As far as I can tell, they were here about six hours ago. You spoke with them when exactly? And they were still here, didn't have any intention of leaving?"

Traci worked hard to recall the conversation, to be accurate then realized her phone tracked the timing of the calls.

"It was four hours ago! They knew I was coming, they were going to stay put, right here. It was the three kids, Mary wasn't doing so good, but they had made it in here, off the highway. They were parked. I told them to stay, I don't understand why they aren't here."

Both Blackie and Traci turned to Sally, who turned to the tech guys sitting at their consoles. "Give me an outside sweep, starting seven hours ago, and put it up over here please"

She pointed to a monitor off to the side.

The screen lit up and images started rolling across. A time lapse, rotating from camera to camera, encompassing the lot, starting with the outside perimeter, then cycling across the interior-facing cams. A ten-minute cycle took about a minute, then it would jump to the next 10 minute segment.

The images weren't sharp, being obscured by the wind driven snow earlier. Shapes and lights could be discerned as they made their way jerkily across the screen. Then they saw it, just pulling into the travel center as a segment ended. A larger shape, not a semi, no definitely not, but smaller. Motor home sized.

The techs noted it and started rolling the video isolating the cameras aimed where it parked. They watched as the snow tapered off, and movement could be seen thru the lighted windows. At one point there was some sort of commotion, but it was very difficult to see clearly what happened. The motorhome door was opposite this view, a different camera's angle showed what MIGHT be the door opening right about when the action occurred. The various feeds were re-run over and over, then Sally said "That's inconclusive, we'll come back to that. Keep rolling ahead."

The wind and blowing snow diminished, the vehicle came more into focus. The sky lightened with the approaching dawn. A figure could clearly be seen walking around it, clearing off the snow. A burly figure, unlike a teen boy. Blackie strained to convince himself he was seeing Nate, but couldn't.

Finally, the RV swung into motion, almost cut off a truck, then drove back onto S Higley Blvd and turned right, southbound. The lower right corner of the screen showed the timestamped; 9:05. TWENTY FIVE minutes ago! About 8 minutes before Traci arrived.

Blackie quickly asked "What's down there?"

"The Wyoming State Penitentiary."

Traci and Blackie exchanged a single glance before he abruptly grabbed her hand and they bolted for the door.

CHAPTER TWENTY EIGHT
THEM PESKY KIDS

Nate's mind raced; what the hell was going ON! What could he DO? What SHOULD he do? The vehicle rocked back and forth as Maynard manhandled them onto the road. The boy put a hand on the dash to brace himself when they turned right and drove beyond the truck stop. Past any remaining remnant of civilization. The snow-covered desert spread out before them. The boy spotted an ominous sign "Wyoming State Penitentiary 2 miles". His anxiety ratcheted even higher. What does THAT mean?

Maynard's thoughts were running wild too. He saw the sign; TWO MILES. He MADE it! Well, yeah, he almost made it, he was gonna make it, he could SEE it almost, just ahead. His confidence had faltered for an instant, when it looked bleak, like Mother goddam Nature was gonna beat him. But no, he punched thru all that crap and now he's HERE!

He glanced over at the kid in the passenger seat; he was staring at Maynard all bug-eyed and shit. Fucking hostages, that's the situation now. Wasn't the way he planned it, no sir, but that plan went off the rails back in DENVER! No time to do more than react since then, he had to go with the flow, go with the... now what, kidnapping? I guess. Pretty much snatched 'em. So at last he gave a passing thought to how this was gonna play out.

The visitation process involved a bunch of advance mumbo-jumbo. Fat Jake's lawyer made the arrangements. Told Maynard to be at the administration building 9:30AM this goddam morning. He glanced at the clock; 9:10. Nice. All white-bread, model citizen-like early and shit. He double-checked his appearance in the mirror; eh, he looked like shit, couldn't do nothing much to improve his mug. But by god, he could paste a smile on his face, a real one, knowing what the looming payoff meant.

But them pesky kids. And granmaw in back. Well, Willie better sit on 'em tight, while Maynard was inside. If they didn't fuck things up, he'd let 'em go. Afterwards. Most likely. He wasn't opposed to killing, he'd put his share of bodies in shallow graves, but this group didn't deserve that. Not yet. Not so far anyway. Not if they were smart and kept quiet, just for a goddam hour or so.

With the decision made, to conditionally spare the lives of his four captives, he refocused on the approaching outer ring of the prison complex.

"Not a peep out any of 'em, you hear me!"

Willie looked at the girl across from him, frowning, his eyes drilling into Elsie's. He answered "Roger that boss."

She saw a flicker of movement overhead as the curtain parted in the upper bunk. Lou peeked out and spotted her sister, smiled and gave a little wave. Elsie's flash of recognition, of surprise, couldn't be hidden from Willie. He grunted and started to stand, pivoting around to see into the compartment above.

Nate saw the movement, heard the grunt, and saw Maynard scowl and turn towards the back. The boy's gut instinct took over as he realized THIS was his moment!

Without thinking, he grabbed the steering wheel and jerked it sharply to the right. Maynard was unable to react quickly enough, and the RV lurched into the snow filled ditch on that side. The occupants were thrown in the opposite direction.

Maynard's head thumped the door, hard. The boy crashed into the driver, elbow first, smacking the man's head against the window a second time. Elsie slid onto the floor, Willie bounced off a small cabinet, hitting his head.

Lou, being in a compressed area, rolled against the side of

the upper bunk and smacked her head against the wall.

As the motorhome pitched nose down into the right-hand ditch, it came to an abrupt stop, jerking the occupants one final time.

When all movement stopped, a brief silence followed. Willie was out cold, Maynard G was slowly coming to, shaking his head. Nate had fallen onto the floor between the seats and lay motionless. Lou was silent behind the closed curtains in the loft.

Maynard had smacked his head pretty hard, twice. Really hard, his ears were ringing. It took a moment to clear his thoughts, to recall events. The meeting and the trip to get there, the storm, the RV, the. . . THE STUPID FUCKING KID GRABBED THE GODDAMN WHEEL!! That kid, right next to his seat!

He scrambled to his feet in a fit of rage, made difficult by the slope of the floor, and lifted his foot to stomp the boy's head hard.

Nate rolled away, maneuvering around Elsie's torso, also in motion, as the two kids clawed their way upright, moving towards the rear, away from the enraged hoodlum.

Willie took that opportunity to start to twitch and jerk on the floor, 'flop like a crappie', with guttural sounds rolling forth.

Maynard was momentarily distracted, taking a second to assess his companion. His attention then returned to the teenagers, who were still edging uphill, away from him.

Suddenly, the bedroom door opened. Mary was barely on her feet, struggling to stand in the doorway, blinking her eyes, taking in the menacing pair, one of them currently in the throes of a seizure. She snapped.

"Who the HELL are you!" she said "and WHAT the HELL is going on?"

Maynard pawed at his sport coat before realizing he wasn't carrying, he was in his law enforcement security-screening civilian costume. But Willie had a piece, probably more than one. And he was right there, all he had to do was bend down, reach inside the jacket of the still-convulsing form of his hapless minion and...

Mary saw the moves, realized he was reaching for the loser-on-the-floor's weapon because he didn't have one. She processed the scene, the odds on potential outcomes, and made her own move.

She had downhill momentem behind the swinging, soccer-style kick delivered to the side of Maynard's head. She was aiming for his hand or arm or shoulder, somewhere a little lower, but he unwittingly moved his noggin into the arc of her bare foot.

She lost her balance with the impact and dropped to the floor. Maynard took the blow on the same spot already aching from kissing the door. Twice. This third time had an immediate result; night-night big fella.

The old woman was pressed against the two thugs, flat on her back. Elsie quickly crossed over, "Mary oh my GOD Mary, are you OK? I can't BELIEVE it, what you did like that, ya kicked him in the HEAD, my god.. c'mon, Mary you OK Mary?"

Thankfully she hadn't lost consciousness, but the old woman was a little loopy. She gradually focused her eyes on the girl, with effort, and gave her a quick smile.

"I think so, I, it seems like I'm OK" She adjusted herself and started to sit up. She shook each of her limbs in turn. "Yes, yes, everything still moves, still attached seems like but OUCH, OW! my foot!"

Elsie and Nate let out a laugh, relieved that she was ok. Her timing, how she showed up and took decisive action, hell, HEROIC action to knock the bad guy out. A kick to the freaking head. They stood awkwardly over Mary and then spontaneously embraced each other in the emotion of the moment. The hormones that generated that hug had been simmering for several days, unacknowledged by either teen. Til then.

Mary grinned at the display of affection between the blushing teens, and reached up. "A little help please?"

They broke apart and gave Mary an assist to her feet. Once upright, her arms encircled the kids in a group hug, holding them silently in the disabled vehicle.

A rustling sound across the room intruded on their upbeat moment. Elsie let out a gasp when she looked over at the noise.

In a rasping voice Willie blurted out "You're DEAD, yer all, DEAD!"

CHAPTER TWENTY NINE
BUCKLE UP TOOTS

Blackie was surprised at the speed they achieved. BAM, out the door and BAM, into the hallway, all with the rather fetching Aunt Traci in tow. She was a trooper, matching him stride for stride as they flew thru the customer service area. A brief pause to get oriented and then the pair blew past several startled shoppers and thru a checkout. In a moment, they're outside in the parking lot. His Ford was closest to the door.

"C'mon, we'll take mine."

He dropped her hand to grab his remote and toggled the locks. He opened the passenger door for her as a gentleman should. Traci tried to remember the last time a man held a door for her and drew a blank. She flopped into the seat as Angus closed her door and dashed to the driver's side.

"It's a rental." he said distractedly, getting the truck fired up and backed out.

She smiled. Duh.

"I spoke with your son you know, around three this morning. He's quite the boy. It's apparent that the girls think the world of Nate. They had quite an adventure, those three."

Blackie had slid the truck into drive but kept his foot on the brake after she said that. He thought back on his journey so far and grimly returned Traci's smile.

"Buckle up Toots; we're in the adventure now too!"

He swiftly swung them around, towards the boulevard and hardly slowed as he turned south, away from town, the same direction the recording showed the RV taking.

They both saw the sign at the same moment, Wyoming State Penitentiary! It was true! He felt his stomach do a flop – A Prison! Traci's reaction was an audible "Oh No!"

The road had been plowed but was covered with an inch or two of white. The wind had dropped to occasional gusts, which tossed a blanket of loose snow and obscured the view ahead. He wanted to drive like a maniac, but after yesterday's accident and all, he couldn't be stupid, couldn't mess this up. But that lead might be 7 or 8 minutes, he just had to cut into it.

Although he couldn't imagine a big old RV making 50 or even 60 miles an hour on this road in the shape it's in, they could be miles ahead. He needed to close the gap but couldn't lose control. A quick glance to the right showed Traci straining against her seatbelt, leaning forward.

Peering ahead, he saw a track, a fresh-looking track, filled in for a stretch or two but reappearing, a track that showed dual wheels. He couldn't recall if the smallest motorhomes would have dualleys, but he'd bet those were the ones! That had to be them. And close!

"See those, those two tracks on each side? That's them! I'm sure that's them!"

Traci nodded, she saw 'em. She glanced at Angus and gave his arm a quick squeeze. He smiled back.

There! On the right, a little ways ahead. A big vehicle. Oh no, it's off the road, in the ditch! NO!

A gasp from Traci.

"It's THEM! Oh Angus, an accident, they CRASHED!"

Blackie pulled to a stop 10 yards behind the RV but still on the road. Traci threw her door open and took off towards the Winnebago yelling "Elsie, LOU!"

A single loud voice was heard inside, a deep voice. A stranger's voice, a man's voice. An angry man. Traci halted suddenly as Blackie caught up to her.

##

The kids had frozen at Willie's murderous threat. Mary

started to say something, to be defiant, to deflect his attention away and he growled and jabbed the gun in her direction.

"You first old woman? Is that how you want it?"

He got to his feet, a little unsteady at first, then very unsteady.

A groan from Maynard diverted Willie's attention. Oh yeah, please wake up boss, take over he thought, I'm not doing so good.

"Boss, can ya hear me? Boss? It's me, Willie. Boss!" He put a hand on Maynard's shoulder, gave it a slight shake. "Boss, hey Boss!"

Someone was coming! The sound of a car outside and now they were approaching on foot. Voices!

As Elsie, Nate and Mary alternately watched the door and Willie's attempts to bring his capo back to conciseness, a new sound emerged. The soft sound of the loft curtains as they were slid back. By Lou. Her shaking hand emerged holding the pistol, pointed up, towards the ceiling.

Willie heard the noise, realized WHO was making it, and over-reacted as he was prone to do.

"Goddammit girlie, GET DOWN HERE!"

No response. He let loose a loud growl, followed with a huge punch – BOOM - to the bottom of the loft. That was a mistake. Because the panicked youngster holding the loaded pistol overhead squeezed the trigger in response. An involuntary reflex, completely understandable.

Our first gunshot.

In the close confines of the motor home, the explosion was overwhelming. The noise and the flash of light threw everyone into shock. Essentially rendered deaf, the interior filled with smoke and eyes began to water . Traci's screams of "ELSIE! LOUISE! GIRLS!" and her pounding and shaking the locked door went unnoticed by the traumatized occupants.

Lou flinched immediately and lost her grip. The gun dropped to the floor, right at Nate's feet. Acting in a soundless trance, in what seemed like super slow motion, he bent down to retrieve it.

Maynard and Willie were not as shell-shocked as the others, having quite a bit of experience with guns and mayhem both in and out of vehicles. They reacted quickly and started to rise, Willie with his gun in his good hand but struggling with his footing.

Mary noticed the door handle shaking and stepped across to unlock it. Blackie and Traci stumbled in, becoming the 7th and 8th occupants inside Mary's Winnebago.

Blackie's worst fears were realized, that the goddam GUN that he'd been so irresponsible with, WAS found, WAS involved, hell, WAS just FIRED, My God! He looked around, worried sick that someone was shot, that injury or even death had resulted.

He took in the scene still hazy with smoke. There was Nate! No blood and, uh oh, the boy was straightening up, he had that goddam gun- in his hand! Blackie's peripheral vision took in the rest of the scene.

One sister, gathered in Traci's arms over in the dinette area. Mary, leaning up against a counter. And Nate! That left one girl unaccounted for. Looking for her, he saw the two thugs.

They were up front in the captain's chairs, at the 'bottom' of the tilted vehicle. And what the hell, one was brandishing his own gun! He swung that barrel across Traci, her niece, then across the old woman. Still moving, it moved past Blackie, and finally stopped, drawing a bead on Nate!

"NOOO, Nate!"

Without thinking, Blackie jumped. The gunman

instinctively altered his aim and fired.

Our second gunshot.

Angus's sense of time distorted. Trigger pulled, the projectile left the gun. He tracked the leisurely revolutions of the bullet as it flew in a perfectly straight line towards him and then watched it punch a hole in his upper left arm. BOOM. The impact twisted him to the left followed by a numbing blow that resonated thru his whole body. Odd he thought, so that's what it's like to get shot.

The sound of the second shot arrives, rendering everyone inside deaf as an even deafer post than before.

Suddenly, a third shot, Nate's shot, which found it's mark. The bad man's weapon flew out of his hand, just like in the movies. Well, to be precise, he pretty much shot Willie's thumb and finger off, the digits flying here, the gun flying there. More gunsmoke, more noise.

"DAD, DAD!" Nate rushed over to Angus, now on the floor, right hand covering an oozing hole in his arm. Blackie read the boy's lips.

"Jesus Nate, am I ever glad to see YOU! Ow, my arm!" He was grinning from ear to ear while lying flat in a growing puddle of blood.

Of course, third gunshot, hearing impairment, neither heard the other's words but the emotions were exchanged.

The boy returned his Father's smile. He couldn't believe how FANTASTIC it was to see the old man again. Friday's dash from Rochester seemed an eternity ago. Nate looked back at Willie and Maynard as he covered them with the pistol.

Willie was bleeding profusely. Maynard's face was beet red, his blood pressure spiking, knowing that his plan lay in ruins.

Lou dropped down out of the loft and joined Traci and Elsie in a big old hug. Mary was on the floor pressing a rag on Blackie's arm.

"Hey bitches, what about ME? I'm bleeding here, geez that hurts! HEY! OVER HERE!"

No one gave a crap about Willie because the SWAT teams sent from the prison just a half mile down the road had arrived. Several officers jammed inside the extremely crowded motor home and efficiently sorted out who was naughty and who was nice. All the occupants were brought outside for appropriate processing.

CHAPTER THIRTY
NOW WHAT?

Angus, Mary and Willie ended up in the Rawlins hospital. Two heroes, the other under armed guard, his remaining fully fingered but suffering severe glass cuts hand cuffed to the bed.

Traci and the kids were guests at the best hotel the Wyoming town had to offer, a Hampton Inn, courtesy of the local Salvation Army. They got to know one another better, enjoying the pool while waiting for the others.

The media swarmed around for the first couple of days, national media, but once all the possible drama was exhausted, the news cycle move on, to an earthquake in a foreign land.

Mary was released first, on Wednesday. Blackie, a day later.

They laughed at the news segments that aired - 'Shootout at the state Pen!!' while getting so many details wrong. Various investigators came by, asking endless questions and compiling their sworn statements. Nate was relieved that no one chose to pursue his theft of the plates in Nebraska; being the hero had it's benefits.

The boy spent time with at the hospital with the others,

some of it alone with his father. Neither one broached the subject of what came next. They talked about everything but that, content to let the future sort itself out.

Nate had been in touch with Sam. She was recovering from a concussion and broken arm. Discharged, her and Colleen were home, taking it easy. The girl was unable to travel; had vertigo, trouble standing and walking. She had half-heartedly pressed Nate about coming down, completing the trip.

Colleen bit her tongue, even as she contemplated a teenaged boy, a total stranger, appearing in their already chaotic home. She directed silent negative vibes at him, urging 'STAY AWAY!'

That's what he did. He stalled Sam, put off giving a definitive answer, blamed it on 'the cops' or 'Dad's doctors'. She struggled, knowing he was with 'that runaway', but she didn't press him too much. She wasn't herself, was still messed up, couldn't hang with Nate like she wanted to, not like this.

The connection to Sam was a struggle for him too. at first. A small and diminishing sense of guilt still nagged at him, as their calls and texts tapered off over the course of several days. They both moved on. Sam focused on her therapy while Nate had a growing interest of his own.

He REALLY enjoyed being with the girls, especially Elsie. It was exciting, and new. He could tell she felt the same way.

It was obvious to the others, the teen's changing relationship. The adults thought it was cute. Lou was torn. The sisterly bond was something strong they'd had forever but it was changing now. She was happy for Elsie and it was fascinating to observe.

Angus and Traci had made the necessary arrangements to be away from their respective homes during this madness. Neither one really had any dependencies back there, no kids or pets. She could offload her grooming work easily and did so.

Mary was diagnosed with pneumonia and put on antibiotics. After her stay in the hospital to get stabilized and hydrated, she joined the others at the motel. The RV was getting three bullet holes patched at a local body shop along with a general once over. The events of the previous days were fading as new realities developed.

Friday evening, all six of them were finally together at the hotel. They sat down in the breakfast area next to the lobby to share an assortment of pizzas. It was a happy time.

Angus sat at the head of the table. He took in the smiling group before him; Mary, the sisters, his son Nate, and the lovely Traci. All thrown together most unexpectedly over the course of a weekend and now so close. He rose to his feet, and with his good right arm, lifted his can of Coke, waiting for silence.

"Can you believe this, all of us here, together, all OK? After what we've been through, it's crazy!"

"All OK says the man with a bullet in his arm!" Nate was quick on the comeback.

Laughter all around. Angus clarified things.

"In and OUT of the arm Nate, past tense. But how about that? We are so blessed, just to be alive and to have found each other."

He took in the group each in turn. Mary, on the mend after her medical treatment, getting her repaired Winnebago back in two more days. Traci or more accurately Traci-and-the-girls. The three of them were already a close unit, a family unit. The girls soaked up Traci's attention, with whispered exchanges and fun outings. For her part, Traci relished this opportunity to fulfill a mothering role, especially to girls their ages.

She also welcomed the addition of the two males in her life. The boy took the girls under his protection at a vulnerable time and she was so grateful. His Dad was also of growing interest to Traci; the way he grabbed her hand, had opened the door, the occasional look between them. It was thrilling.

Elsie was electrified and happy and awkward and self-conscious all at the same time. Because Traci was so wonderful, and Mom was stabilized back in Omaha, going thru rehab, everything was all good now. Especially Nate! She felt flushed when they were together and couldn't stop thinking of him when they were apart. It was so different, so delightful!

The younger sister was quiet, more so than normal. There was a lot to process, so much drama so fast. And the endless loop playing in her head where Willie hit the bunk and she pulled the trigger. Over and over, punch, BOOM. It was weird the power the gun had, the recoil, the SURPRISE! punch, BOOM.

Added to that was the developing storyline of her sister and Nate, PLUS Aunt Traci arriving and offloading responsibility from Elsie. Lou took a lot of comfort from her presence. She picked up on the vibes between Angus and her Aunt too, an interesting development itself.

Nate was in the same state of mind as Elsie; jacked on hormones. That girl was ninety percent of his focus at any one time now, which kept him in an growing haze. Sam didn't enter his thoughts at all, she was working on a needed recovery down in Vegas, had her Mom for support. Of course, Nate had his Dad now too, who was in recovery and also needed attention.

The boy was still amazed and shocked that Angus showed up. Grateful that he'd come after him, somewhat guilty that Dad had stepped in to take the bullet aimed at Nate. OK, real guilty! Thanks Pop!

"A toast, to us!" Angus offered his Coke. Raised glasses all around, 'Here here!' and 'Toast!'

Lou had a different thought.

"Now what?"

Her words deflated the mood rather quickly. The others realized the need to address what comes next. The road trip, bad guys, gunfire, publicity and recovery, all that was now behind them. What was in front?

Angus knew. It came to him in a dream last night, where they'd be in six months, what came after the pizza party in Rawlins Wyoming.

He'd seen Mary taking it easy in a Spanish Fork condo. The one Traci owned. Traveling in a motor home had lost its charm and Mary had it up for sale.

The condo was just the right size for a single person. It was home to Traci for years, she owned it free and clear. Small and neat, single bedroom, ideal for a down-sized individual like Mary.

Too small to accommodate someone with a couple of young girls. Once Traci was granted temporary custody of Elsie and Lou during their mother's year long rehab, a new residence was needed. One large enough for a good-sized family unit. Several adults, teens, and a pre-teen. Maybe in a rural setting, perhaps in Southern Minnesota.

And that's how things turned out. Angus and Traci shared a bedroom, the kids each had their own. School had ended, the summer beckoned.

Angus got the call from Colleen in Las Vegas on June 1st.

"Sam flipped out and stole my car Angus! She's on the run, to Minnesota, to Nate!"

THE END

308

Made in the USA
Monee, IL
27 December 2019